ISLAND CREATURES

ALSO BY MARGARITA ENGLE

*also available in Spanish

Enchanted Air:
Two Cultures, Two Wings: A Memoir

The Firefly Letters:
A Suffragette's Journey to Cuba

Forest World

Hurricane Dancers:
The First Caribbean Pirate Shipwreck

Jazz Owls
A Novel of the Zoot Suit Riots

The Lightning Dreamer:
Cuba's Greatest Abolitionist

Lion Island:
Cuba's Warrior of Words

The Poet Slave of Cuba:
A Biography of Juan Francisco Manzano

Rima's Rebellion:
Courage in a Time of Tyranny

Silver People:
Voices from the Panama Canal

Soaring Earth:
A Companion Memoir to Enchanted Air

The Surrender Tree:
Poems of Cuba's Struggle for Freedom

Tropical Secrets:
Holocaust Refugees in Cuba

The Wild Book

Wild Dreamers

Wings in the Wild

With a Star in My Hand:
Rubén Darío, Poetry Hero

Your Heart, My Sky:
Love in a Time of Hunger

MARGARITA ENGLE

ISLAND CREATURES

atheneum

NEW YORK AMSTERDAM/ANTWERP LONDON
TORONTO SYDNEY/MELBOURNE NEW DELHI

atheneum

An imprint of Simon & Schuster Children's Publishing Division
1230 Avenue of the Americas, New York, New York 10020

For more than 100 years, Simon & Schuster has championed authors and the stories they create. By respecting the copyright of an author's intellectual property, you enable Simon & Schuster and the author to continue publishing exceptional books for years to come. We thank you for supporting the author's copyright by purchasing an authorized edition of this book.

No amount of this book may be reproduced or stored in any format, nor may it be uploaded to any website, database, language-learning model, or other repository, retrieval, or artificial intelligence system without express permission. All rights reserved. Inquiries may be directed to Simon & Schuster, 1230 Avenue of the Americas, New York, NY 10020 or permissions@simonandschuster.com. This book is a work of fiction. Any references to historical events, real people, or real places are used fictitiously. Other names, characters, places, and events are products of the author's imagination, and any resemblance to actual events or places or persons, living or dead, is entirely coincidental.

Text © 2025 by Margarita Engle

Jacket illustration © 2025 by Alex Cabal

Jacket design by Rebecca Syracuse

All rights reserved, including the right of reproduction in whole or in part in any form.

Atheneum logo is a trademark of Simon & Schuster, LLC.

For information about special discounts for bulk purchases, please contact Simon & Schuster Special Sales at 1-866-506-1949 or business@simonandschuster.com.

Simon & Schuster strongly believes in freedom of expression and stands against censorship in all its forms. For more information, visit BooksBelong.com.

The Simon & Schuster Speakers Bureau can bring authors to your live event. For more information or to book an event, contact the Simon & Schuster Speakers Bureau at 1-866-248-3049 or visit our website at www.simonspeakers.com.

Interior design by Rebecca Syracuse

The text for this book was set in Charter.

Manufactured in the United States of America

First Edition

10 9 8 7 6 5 4 3 2 1

Library of Congress Cataloging-in-Publication Data

Names: Engle, Margarita, author.

Title: Island creatures / Margarita Engle.

Description: First edition. | New York : Atheneum Books for Young Readers, 2025. | Audience: Ages 12 up. | Audience: Grades 7–9. | Summary: Cuban childhood friends Vida and Adán rediscover each other in Florida where they work together to protect endangered animals while navigating their complicated homelives.

Identifiers: LCCN 2024018379 (print) | LCCN 2024018380 (ebook) | ISBN 9781665959957 (hardcover) | ISBN 9781665959971 (ebook)

Subjects: CYAC: Novels in verse. | Zoos—Fiction. | Family life—Fiction. | Cuban Americans—Fiction. | Romance stories. | LCGFT: Novels in verse. | Romance fiction.

Classification: LCC PZ7.5.E54 Is 2025 (print) | LCC PZ7.5.E54 (ebook) | DDC [Fic]—dc23

LC record available at https://lccn.loc.gov/2024018379

LC ebook record available at https://lccn.loc.gov/2024018380

for endangered animals
and the rare people who stay with them
during hurricanes
and for feminists of any gender

ISLAND CREATURES

TEN YEARS AGO

Guamuhaya Mountains
central Cuba

ISLAND CHILDHOOD

the children roamed rough trails on green peaks
where wild rivers were born above waterfalls
that plunged down to deep blue pools
filled with reflections
of wishful
legends

each time the boy saw horses
hauling loads that were too heavy
or a team of weary oxen straining
beneath their shared wooden yoke
or a dog beaten for frenzied barking
or sad songbirds caged as curiosities
he released the tormented beings
then led them to a fragrant cacao farm
where they were tended by a girl
who gave the creatures food
and music, songs she invented
to make life seem
serene

NOW

suburban South Florida

RARE AND ENDANGERED
Vida

When I sing to wounded animals
my voice grows, rises, and flows
like feathery wings with lives
of their own
separate
from
me.

I
am
just a flutter
of lovely words in scented air
drifting toward the steep waterfall
of memories that I almost want to forget
and just as passionately hope to keep.

ALIVE
Vida

After I survived the plague of dengue fever
that seized my parents, Abuelita Rita came
and changed my name from Serena to Vida
in honor of life.

She brought me here to a pink house in Miami
where I learned English, Spanglish, photography,
and the survivor's art of pretending to believe
that I am strong
and courageous.

Rita could easily retire,
but she chooses to keep working
and traveling as a photojournalist,
thrilled by all the new digital wizardry
that helps her document horrific atrocities
along with inspiring acts of human kindness
in war zones and deforested moonscapes
all over the world.

Her collection of old cameras
with immense telescopic lenses
is mine now

and so is the closet
she converted into a darkroom
where mystifying chemicals
transform ghostly negatives
into breathtaking images
that I can hold
in my hands
flat
tangible
proof
of light's ability
to make life's shadows
visible and solid, contained within
the walls, ceilings, and floors
of angular
frames.

SURVIVE
Vida

I research the word's origin
and learn that it means *super alive*
from the combined Latin roots
of *above*
and *to live*.

Etymology helps me feel superheroic,
at least in my memory of those moments
when the boy Catey and I helped living creatures
rise above the deep pool
of a shimmering
future.

AWAKE
Vida

Daydreams and memories
are equally vivid in daylight.

I remember things that seem true
but could have been imagined
depending on whether
there is a tidy frame
inside my mind
to contain
the lost past
when I was little,
so bold and confident,
in love with el monte,
green trees, a waterfall,
fragile creatures, the scent of cacao,
and the smile of el niño Catey.

Whenever we rescued animals
our minds left the ground, lifting us up
to float like clouds.

ALONE
Vida

While Abuelita Rita travels all over the world
photographing battles, famines, and festivals,
I remain at home, solitary, determined to fill out
applications for summer jobs that might allow me
to feel vibrant
outdoors
in sunlight.

No matter how long I live here
in this sprawling city of pink houses
and exiled islanders, I still feel weightless
whenever my mind rises up to dance
in the tender embrace
of time.

I think of the boy, his dimpled smile
and gentle courage—without him, so many
suffering creatures would have forgotten
that humans
can be merciful.

the children invented
their own silent language
of leaps and pirouettes
a way of dancing
with winged beings
and four-legged ones
who depended on them
for kindness

every animal they rescued
was given a safe place to live

a new home
with strangers
who came from far away
just to help the girl and boy
turn daydreams
into real life

her parents approved
because they had always believed
that their cacao farm was a magical crop
rooted in chocolate's aroma of generosity

EXODUS
Adán

As a child I was called Catey—
the Taíno way of saying *parakeet*—
in honor of all the small, caged birds
that Serena and I released when we
were expert creature thieves.

Then our mountain's climate changed abruptly.
Drought killed cacao trees, floods were followed
by landslides, and because chocolate is a sweet crop
that should never be grown in cruel places,
we had no way to thrive, no more candy to sell
to foreigners in fancy tourist shops.

Mosquitoes swarmed, a Biblical plague
filled with diseases both new and old:
zika, chikungunya, malaria, yellow fever,
and hemorrhagic dengue, a horrifying virus
that makes people bleed from their skin, ears,
even eyes.

Serenita's parents died swiftly
and she would have been next
but her abuela Rita arrived just in time

to take her away
leaving
        my
seven-year-old heart
    shattered.

Now that I'm grown
it's almost impossible for me to believe
that I fell in love
so long ago.

FORTRESS
Vida

Sometimes I'm so fearful
that I can't allow myself to be
spontaneous.

I crave plans
escape routes
survival strategies
ways to protect
my emotions.

A life of loss
has taught me
caution.

Once, when I had to write a poem
about who I am, in an English class
where everyone else seemed happy,
I chose the title: "Architecture"
then added
a fortress
built
of light.

I think of my future
as a photograph's
shadow.

FREE FALL
Adán

Béisbol has shown me how to never hesitate.
There's no point wondering whether my first base run
was fast enough
once I'm already
sliding
toward
home.

So I hit
race
hope.

Coach
calls me
a skydiver.

JOURNEY FROM HOME TO HOME
Adán

My whole family rowed a small boat to Florida
at a time when wet feet from the sea meant that we
were allowed to stay here in the mythical US
and become citizens—still desperately poor
but more or less free to hope for prosperity.

Our house is rented
and crowded, noisy
with my sisters' voices,
Mami and Abuela's lively stories,
Papi and Abuelo's loud arguments
about their efforts to make a living
as landscape gardeners . . .

but sometimes I miss the colorful cacao pods,
and that scent of raw pulp before the process
of transformation from seeds to chocolate,
and every day I miss Serena and her parents,
the only people who truly knew my secret skill
as a rescuer of animals who needed
their own form of freedom.

SUMMER JOB DREAMS
Adán

Possibilities
shimmer and blink
on my laptop
screen.

In the past, I've worked with Papi and Abuelo
as a gardener, or with Coach, teaching baseball
to little kids, but now I crave something new—
camp counselor at a breeding zoo
where children will see how rare species
can be rescued, their descendants
eventually rewilded
to natural habitats.

It's an intricate way to feel free
in this harsh world
of rigid
cages.

INTERSPECIES POETRY CLUB
Vida

Every day after school
instead of languishing in an empty house
while Rita is in Crimea, Burkina Faso, or Peru
I read out loud
to lonely animals
at a wildlife rescue center
where wings and legs heal
while lost hopes
are found.

Dulce María Loynaz is the owls' favorite poet.
They love the short verses from *Bestiarium*
and longer ones from *Poemas sin nombre*,
like that poem about island creatures,
island rivers, and island stones,
all so light and nimble
that they rise
and fly.

It's as if la poeta knew me and Catey
when we floated above Cuba's cage of waves.

READING NAMELESS POEMS OUT LOUD

Vida

Dulce María Loynaz was censored in Cuba,
unable to publish after the revolution
because she wrote about love and flowers
instead of war and power.

After she died
her home became a cultural center
with a huge sculpture in the courtyard
of a headless woman without a mouth
or voice.

Now, while injured owls and eagles listen,
my own voice soars to meet la poeta's
musical language
in midair.

Poems don't need names
when the audience is an assortment
of winged creatures who have never learned
any words.

POTION
Vida

When you work with animals
the whole world is made of invisible
particles, floating aromas that wrap
molecules
around you
an elixir
of fur
feathers
breath
digestion . . .

So I read to wild creatures
knowing my clothes stink from owl pellets
and bat guano, but the smells remind me
that all the animals and I are
alive
alive
alive!

We are
survivors.

RESCUE
Adán

I'm on my way home
from a night game (we won!)
when I see a small dog chained
to the outside of a gate.

Strange.
Why not the inside?
People who are cruel to animals
usually want to keep them cooped up.

I park.
Peer all around.
No flashlight needed.
There's a bit of a moon.
Security cameras?
I'll take my chances.

Freeing a captive creature helps me feel
hopeful, just like my younger self, the boy
called Catey, who levitated in mountains
as fragrant as bittersweet chocolate.

NOT A DOG AFTER ALL
Adán

I cut the chain
free the creature
wrap it in a blanket
and run to my truck.

He's a gray tree fox, the kind that climbs
and makes so many wild, eerie sounds—
catlike yowls, a canine whine, yips, barks,
explosive growls.

But this zorro is silent
except for his lapping tongue
as he soothes the thirst he must have endured
for hours, chained to a gate by a sadistic human
who wanted death
to be slow and painful.

I'll report the guy for sure.
Cruelty to animals
is a crime.

SANCTUARY

Adán

The lights are on.
A veterinarian is here!

There's also a girl around my age
with dark chocolate hair that ripples
over her shoulders, and a curvy shape,
and wide green eyes
in a dark honey face
just like Serena's gaze
when we were little . . .

but the name tag
on this hot girl's shirt
says *Vida—Life*—such an unusual name
but it's perfect for a person who comforts
wounded creatures.

HOPE, ALWAYS HOPE
Vida

I smell the guy who rescued the fox
right before I look up and see his muscles
and sweet smile—dimples, shaggy black hair,
skin the reddish brown of cinnamon, and there must be
pheromones in sweat, because I feel just as attracted
as if he were shirtless, instead of covered
in a dirty baseball uniform,
mud on his chest and sleeves,
knees, thighs . . .

If there's an award for worst flirting skills
I'll win, because I've always been unable
to master chatty bantering, so instead
I just listen to the veterinarian
as she recites injuries, dehydration,
abrasions from the chain, fear, terror, trauma,
and hope, always hope, in this case
a high probability that the fox will survive
and be released into the wild
alive, alive, alive!

each creature they rescued
felt magical to the children
who saw the animals
as guardian angels
instead of the other
way around

LEVITATION
Adán

Once the fox is safe
and settled in a crate
I stay and listen
to the soothing music
of Vida's rhythmic voice
as she reads to birds
her words
      stirring
   swirls
     of my wistful   memorias.

Whenever my friend Serena sang
to las criaturas that we rescued together
I always felt myself lifted by la música.

Now I feel it again, that ability to transcend
all the clutter that tries to capture my mind
and hold me hostage.

Heart in the air   my imagination
               floats.

SECOND ENCOUNTER
Vida

The fox needs care
these owls crave poetry
and all I want is freedom to dream
of a time when the word *man*
was not yet a synonym
for *danger*.

It's Saturday, no school, and halfway
through this quiet morning, Adán returns
with his little sister, Albalucía,
who says she prefers
to be called Luci.

She uses a wheelchair.
One of her legs is short and twisted.
Polio, she admits with a shrug, because her parents
decided not to have her vaccinated after they reached
the US, so now she lives with the consequences,
but her pain isn't constant; quite often,
she's able to walk with crutches
or just a cane.

MEMORY QUIZ
Vida

As if to help her brother ask questions
Luci volunteers her own answers
announcing that she can guess
how I choose poems to read out loud
to my audience of animals.

My eyes wander from her animated face
to her brother's almost-familiar
dark eyes
and dimpled grin.

I already feel like I know him again
even though we haven't spoken
about our childhood names.
He's Catey.
I'm Serena.
We're bold little creature thieves
transformed into teenage strangers.

The last time I saw Luci, she was a toddler
and her legs were sturdy, healthy, whole.
Now she's an exuberant tween
telling me about her big sisters'

feminist book club
and her brother's earnest efforts
to be an equal rights ally.

She guessed right.
Reading about equality for women
is definitely a point in his favor
as if I needed
one more reason
to remember
and trust
Catey.

ISLA
Adán

Vida's voice
feels like music
as it enters my ears.

Her dark hair is braided today
her form alluring in a sundress
the color of a forest.

If she were made of rocks and sand,
she would vanish beneath the rising sea
of my imagination, then return
mountainous
thunderous
a volcano
alive
aflame.

I've flirted, dated, and so much more
but never with someone who seemed
both real and mysteriously dreamlike
eyes like ferns, curling toward me.

HOW TO TRIUMPH
Vida

Catey was as thin and bony
as the bright green parakeets
he rescued from cages.

This guy is strong
a baseball player with arms
like a superhero, but his face is so familiar
I'm certain he's my childhood friend
long lost and somehow
now found again.

A poem from Ada Limón is next, I announce to the owls
while Adán's little sister smiles her approval
and says "How to Triumph Like a Girl"
is her favorite verse, because she loves horses
and hopes to ride in the Special Olympics someday.

It's easy for me to imagine
her exhilarated
victory!

NAME ME

Adán

The next poem
is also by Ada Limón
but it's a quiet verse
set in the Garden of Eden
where Eve
gives names
to all the animals
while wondering
what they
might
call
her.

I'm not quite ready to tell Vida
that I'm almost sure I remember her, because
what if I'm wrong and she's not really Serenita?
Then she'll assume it's just a pickup line
that I might have used before
over and over, like a spell
guys try to cast on girls.

QUESTIONS ABOUT SPIRITS
Vida

Late at night, alone in my silent house,
I look up the origins of the word *creature*
and find that it grew from *creare*, the Latin
for *create*.

What about my lost parents?
Do the dead still live in some creative way
that I can't see or hear, but can easily imagine?

Is my imagination its own creation
or was my mind made long before I was born?
And do I share thoughts with other creatures
who daydream inside
hidden worlds?

Did I create my memories of Catey
or were we really able to rise up to sky-dance
whenever we held each other's
                        small hands?

REUNITED

Adán

A moment
of definite recognition
occurs right after I've greeted Vida
several times, each conversation
a bit more revealing than the last.

She welcomes me with air-kisses
her lips almost reaching my cheek
as I place my hands on her shoulders
to hold my heart
steady.

Catey, she says.
Serena, I reply.

As soon as we've pronounced
those names from our shared past
we're friends again, as if we'd never
lost the closeness of childhood
in el monte, our green forest
with its aroma of cocoa.

REDISCOVERY
Vida

This embrace
makes me tremble
but instead of fear, I experience
a sense of wonder, because he is not
one of those scary guys—here is my old friend
Catey, a small child grown large and strong
but still trustworthy
and gentle.

So I send my confusion into the silence
as I release only a fragment of the agonizing story
about my parents' deaths, and the way I was adopted
by a grandmother I had never met, a traveler
who is so rarely home that sometimes I feel
even more alone
than when I believed
I was just about to die
and be torn apart
by vultures.

BALANCING ACT
Adán

I listen.
Try to hug her.
She turns away.
Tells me to leave . . .

but my little sister begs, until Vida finally agrees
to watch a riding lesson at the therapeutic stable
where I trade my manure-shoveling labor
for Luci's chance to feel strong and swift
on horseback, at least once each week.

Now it's like I'm perched way up high too,
trying to keep from tumbling off a horse or a cliff,
this rediscovery of my long-lost best friend
as precarious as swimming in el río
too close to the waterfall's roar.
If I tumble,
will I vanish
in a current
of mist?

TRUTH OR DARE
Vida

I help groom the horse
straighten the saddle
tighten the cinch
lift the child.

Perched up high
she challenges me
to a game.

Truth
is too risky
so I choose a dare.

Be brave, Luci demands.
Let my brother be happy.
Give him a chance.
Why are you
so scared?

the boy stole an iguana
from a tourist's backpack
where it was tied up
held captive
as a souvenir

but the girl
was too feverish
to help feed the immense lizard

so the boy stood alone
at the edge of a forest
while he set it free
beside towering
tree ferns

blood seeped from the girl's green eyes
and her fingers felt like flaming torches
but he clutched her hands anyway
hoping to ease her pain by claiming
her dangerous heat
as his own

PEGASUS
Vida

I aim a heavy camera
at the brave little girl as she rides away
my timing
perfect
as doves
flutter
behind her
and a hybrid image emerges, the horse-girl
miraculously winged.

ENTRANCED
Adán

Her camera
and darkroom
are mystical
this framed
photo
magical.

Vida's hair smells like a chemistry lab,
but I'm fascinated, because she claims
there's a golden hour each evening
right before sunset
when reality
and imagination
meet and dance in midair.

Photography, she proclaims, is a quest
for the treasures
of light
outlined
by darkness.

UNCERTAINTY
Vida

Adán is the first guy I've ever invited
into this house.
For ten years, I missed Catey
without realizing that we lived in the same city
just a few miles apart.

Now somehow we've abruptly reclaimed
all our magical possibilities from childhood.
It's not something I can explain with words
so I take a picture of him holding a frame
that will eventually contain his portrait.

I'm dressed sloppy, in shorts and a tank top,
hair wild and tangled, no makeup—but he says
I'm beautiful, and somehow I want to believe him
even though the attention is frightening
this closeness
impossible
to map.

What if he's aggressive like those other guys,
the human bulldozers who almost crushed me?

OLD NAMES AND NEW

Adán

Los cateyes are green birds so lively
and cheerful that people capture them
and keep them as pets, but my real name, Adán,
just means *Adam*, an ancient loner who knows
nothing and is always starting over
the mystical garden around him
entirely new.

Serena belonged to a time when being serene
seemed possible, but Vida is *Life*, complicated
and unpredictable, with emotions that rise
and soar, or plummet
toward depths.

We agree to tell each other the true tales
of our decade here in Florida, each one assuming
that the other was still far away.

We take turns holding an empty photo frame
as we reveal our emotional stories
of exodus and reinvention.

DIARY OF AN ORPHAN
Vida

My grandmother is still a mystery
even after an entire decade together.

Long before I was born, she had fled
the island to become a photojournalist.
After she rescued me from dengue fever
we never spent an entire year in this house.
There were hotels, babysitters, nannies,
then a boarding school where I turned gloomy,
so miserable beneath the scrutiny of strangers
who had no memory of poverty,
privileged rich kids too arrogant
for friendship, boys who asked
if my breasts were real, then reached out
and touched, as if I were a statue.

Sometimes I wished for an old-fashioned abuelita
who would stay home and bake pastelitos
but I'm proud of Rita; her photos are heroic
and she's such a bold example
of feminist
independence.

MY COMPLICATED FAMILY
Adán

My older sisters are college students
who still live at home, to save money.
Graciela wants to be a doctor, and Libertad
is interested in medical research, because
we've all been affected by Luci's polio
and by the way our parents
absorbed anti-vaccination
conspiracy theories
as soon as we arrived
in the mythically free US
where anyone can spread false rumors
and there's no way to identify truth.

Now, Mami spends most of her time
helping my little sister with physical therapy
and tutoring so Luci can try to catch up after years
of poor attendance at school, the result
of pain and weakness.

Papi and Abuelo both drink too much
while Abuela watches telenovelas to avoid
taking sides in machista arguments.

There's nothing more troubling
than being expected to choose
between my father
and grandfather
when both
are wrong.

Men who fight other men
don't seem to notice
that women and children
are the ones whose minds
and memories
get bruised.

War doesn't need a country.
It can rage on and on for years
inside one tiny house.

FIST
Adán

Every time my drunk father and grandfather fight—
as fervently as if they believe their anger is a religion—
I glance down at my own coiled hands
and will myself to remember
how powerfully
and harmlessly
the bat
smacks a ball
while the whole team cheers
spirits lifted as we share
exhilaration.

Human hands
can be so hopeful
but fists
are always
lonely.

NARROW ESCAPE
Vida

The boarding school
had a breeding facility for rare species.
I was one of the students called Zooies,
because I qualified for an internship
where I learned how to care
for endangered sun bears, red pandas,
Andean flamingos, and a baby kangaroo
who rode around in the pocket of my hoodie
as if I were his mother, with a natural pouch.

The tragic part of this story
should have been avoidable.
Security was inadequate, because
administrators refused to see that humans
are far more dangerous
than animals.

One night while I was getting ready to leave
after a vet check of all the flamingos, I was stalked,
ambushed, and assaulted by two drunk seniors
who never worried about consequences
because their surnames were on buildings
all over the campus, their parents wealthy donors

whose word in court would carry so much more
weight
than mine.

I kicked one of the assailants
and bit the other, while pink birds
with clipped wings
cheered me
and tripped
my pursuers
as I raced away, escaping
just in time to avoid being raped . . .

The next day, I dropped out of school,
moved home, and switched to independent study.
Now I volunteer at the wildlife sanctuary,
singing to soothe myself and other
wounded orphans.

The lyrics of my songs are reinvented each day
because I need to feel new and safe,
reborn in solitude.

FRIEND ZONE
Adán

When Vida explains why she's afraid of men
I make up my mind to accept whatever
boundaries she needs.

Platonic amor was enough for us
when we were too little to understand
that there could ever be more, so now
it can be enough again
unless
someday
she's the one
who chooses
to touch
me.

TRUST ZONE
Vida

Abuelita still doesn't know why I was so desperate
to flee that school. She would never leave me alone
for even a moment if I told her about the attempted
attack, and my narrow escape, so I always pretend
that I simply missed living at home.

Now, when I spontaneously tell Adán, I realize
that somehow—even though he's grown so tall,
strong, and calm—to me he's still Catey
short and skinny
shy and funny
a symbol
of safety.

Together we were
creature-rescuing heroes.
We trusted each other completely.

No wonder I feel so certain
that I can trust him again.

WATERFALL
Vida

in dreams
       I
       leap
       toward
       you
       far
       below
       as
       you
       tread
       water
       ready
       to
       swim
       together
in dreams where love is already
a legend in the deep pool
of our past or future
there's no way to tell
the difference
in dreams

BÉISBOL
Vida

I watch Adán play and win,
so glad he chose this familiar game
instead of violent American football
with all those brutal injuries.

Baseball is Cuba's favorite sport
so here in Florida, I think of home runs
as wistful quests for a place to belong.

Each time the umpire cleans home plate
with his little brush
wild birds
flutter
inside
the aviary
of my heart.

the first animals they rescued
were doves, roosters, and goats
intended for sacrifice
during ceremonies
at altars

se enojaron los santeros
but none of the curses
cast as revenge
ever reached
the children
who were guarded
by the spirits of creatures
with leaping legs and flapping wings
that lifted human minds
like night birds
released
from a cavern
of kindness

THE WEIGHT OF AN ISLAND
Adán

when I remember childhood
I feel like Atlas in that Greek myth, lifting mountains
onto my shoulders
both past
and future
a fragrant forest
so heavy that the weight might press me down into waves
as I struggle to cross the fierce sea, carrying la isla
with me

WORDS MADE OF WISHES
Adán

Together, we read out loud to owls, eagles, hawks,
and a scarlet ibis so delicate that he looks like a breeze
could break his wings, even though he's a species
known for courage during hurricanes.

The fox has been released triumphantly
so an orphaned bobcat is now the center
of the veterinarian's attention.

Vida and I take turns choosing poems
from *Absolute Solitude* by Dulce María Loynaz.
There's one that's my favorite, about poets
who would find some way to create new birds
if the real ones suddenly vanished.

Sometimes it's hard to be certain
that I'm really here, instead of back in el monte,
a small child holding his friend's hand

                             as our voices rise up

                                       and we

levitate.

POETRY FOR WOUNDED BIRDS
Vida

our voices rise
like sunlight
and clouds

words
are the only way to escape
life's transparent aviary

any language can fly
as long as the feathery sounds
create music

TIME HOVERS
Adán

Vida photographs all my games
and tonight one of her photos
caught
the airborne pelota
just
as
a
dragonfly passed.

Tomorrow, framed, it will look
                like the baseball
                        is winged

while far below—running, racing, winning—
I'll appear to be an ordinary land animal
                who somehow sent hope   soaring.

MOMENTS
Vida

I've never liked it when people say
photographs capture time.

Time is wild.
Photos are more like reflections
or echoes.

I refuse to think of moments
as zoo beasts
caged
tamed.

LIGHT-YEARS
Adán

Vida, when we were little
and you suddenly vanished,
I folded a paper boat
and sent it floating
down the river
over the falls
to find you . . .

never realizing
how slowly
hope
travels.

Now you seem
so much bolder than before
even though around my teammates
and my sisters you're quiet and shy
unless you're holding a mystical camera
that releases light's courageous blend
of waves and particles, movement
blended with stillness.

KINDNESS IS A PHEROMONE
Vida

Adán, after each of your hermanita's riding lessons
when Luci dances from the waist up, still seated
on the horse, you perch on a fence to join her rumba
without using your feet, so she won't feel alone
in her life
   of physical
      limitations.

I've never kissed any guy voluntarily
but your gentleness is so attractive
that I almost wonder
   if sooner or later
      my lips might
         seek yours.

What if you say no?
I'll be embarrassed, but you are generous
to animals and children, so you probably won't
humiliate me
too much.

WHEN LIPS FINALLY MEET
Vida

time twirls
        inside
            our kiss

spin
       twist
           dizzy

yesterday
    tomorrow
       forever

I dance
      in the arms
            of now

DRIFT

Adán

each airborne kiss
a star in the magical river
reflected

FLYING WHILE FALLING IN LOVE
Vida and Adán

sky
dance

HOW TO SOAR
Adán and Vida

between mind and body
lies a layer of air
and daydreams

fingers
breath
imagination
entwined
we rise
        two lives
            fly

the children were never sure
whether they really could   fly

all they knew
was that friendship
helped their minds rise

                          hearts

                                light

FEARLESS
Vida

unafraid
of lips
eyes
hands

I never imagined
I could ever recover
calm
confidence
so close to any boy or man
but all it takes is love's kindness
to make the whole world
a bit less terrifying

courage is like one of those extinct species
suddenly rediscovered
alive

OPEN SKY
Adán and Vida

hearts follow
        minds
          clouds
             float
                free
and then we return
to our ordinary
miraculous
life
on land

EMBRACE
Vida

from longing to belonging
my cliff-diving heart's
migration

THE ONLY GUY AT A FEMINIST BOOK CLUB
Adán

I'm bursting with hope for time alone with Vida
but my older hermanas insist that I bring her
to their passionate discussion of *The Poet X,*
Brown Girl Dreaming, and *A Time to Dance.*

I hope Elizabeth Acevedo, Jacqueline Woodson,
and Padma Venkatraman will all forgive me
for not quite concentrating on every word
in their powerful verse books, while my mind
keeps slipping back
to that last kiss
and the next one . . .

THE COMPANIONSHIP OF COLLEGE GIRLS
Vida

I'm so relieved
that Adán's twin sisters
accept me, because a decade ago
when I was seven and they were ten
they thought I was so annoying.

All they ever did was babysit little Luci
while I was outdoors with their brother
free to run, jump, climb trees,
and rescue creatures.

Now Graciela and Libertad help me feel
like an almost-adult, as we discuss metaphors,
similes, and the origin of words like *friend*
which stems from the combined roots
of *freedom*
and *love*.

EXPERIMENTAL
Adán

My college sisters don't have boyfriends.
Both say they want to experiment first,
flying swiftly through many relationships
before deciding
where to land.

They're not shy about warning Vida
to take her time choosing a path for her future
but lucky for me
little Luci
disagrees—she tells my novia, over and over,
to just go ahead
and accept me
the way I am.

INSPIRED BY THE
FEMINIST BOOK CLUB
Vida

a circle of girls
and one guy, our ally
as we read and discuss
a shared dream
equality

I think of all the animals that form rings
around their young, to protect against predators.
Musk oxen, bison, horses, even elephants and dolphins
perch in a circle to defend the future.

Old men who imagine that their ancient rules
might survive
have no idea how strong and brave girls
can be
when our circles of loyalty are finally
seen
and our voices find homes
on paper.

ETYMOLOGY
Vida

Adán's sisters are all so sweet to me
that I feel like I could listen to them all day
but as we read poems
the verses lead to searches
for the origins of certain words,
so now we're discussing *poet*
which grew from the Greek for *maker*
a synonym of *artisan,* as if rhymes
are furniture you can build
from slices of forest.

We learn that *kindness* comes from *kinship*
because most people are usually kind to relatives.

Then we look up *feminism*
which turns out to be a term invented
by a man, so everyone agrees that maybe
it's time to dream of some new way to say
justice
for women.

STEMINISM
Vida

We read biographies
of pioneering women scientists
whose accomplishments were usurped
by male colleagues, or husbands, fathers,
brothers . . .

I remember
the loneliness
of life without Adán
who understands both equality
and dendrofeminology, the tree ring calendar
of women's history.
Goddess worship was forbidden
back when ancient forests were seedlings,
then female healers were accused of witchcraft,
and later the daring suffragists were beaten
and mocked, until now, somehow
while those same ancient forests
are dying, women's rights are revoked,
young girls punished
for the simple crime
of hope.

TIME FLOW
Adán and Vida

Later, when we're alone
we talk about every aspect
of each idea
that fills
the air
between
    us
balanced
    above
    love
    friendship
    freedom
equality
    poetry
kindness
    past
and future
    floating toward
        now

COURAGE
Vida

I'm growing accustomed
to thinking of us as a couple of separate
nearly adult individuals, instead of children
who swam naked
so freely
beneath
our familiar
waterfall.

Release from fear
is such an unexpected
relief
that it's easy
to imagine
skinny-dipping
again
someday.

SUPERSTITIOUS
Adán

Love feels both thrilling
and unpredictable, but baseball players
are used to the chance of losing
so we create rituals—I never cut my hair
during béisbol season, just in case the old story
about Samson turns out to be even a little bit true.

Now, as if making a new constellation in the sky,
I draw Vida's name above my heart, like a tattoo.

Each time I see her in the stands, wearing
my team colors, gold and blue, I'm stunned
by the way she looks like sun and sky,
warmth and light, hope for the flight
of a moon shot
home run
long
and
high.

NIGHT FLIGHT
Vida

When Adán is on third base
he leaps to catch the soaring pelota.

The next day, I frame a silhouette
that shows
his
fingers
clasped around a sphere.

Ball, moon, or star
anyone who sees this picture
will feel free to choose
their own
belief.

when the boy finally realized
that the girl was really gone
he crafted a tightly wrapped ball
of soggy string
and whacked it with a stick
furious
powerful

but the ball floated away in a muddy flood
and the stick drifted over the waterfall
soon everything was lost
to climate disaster and disease, until finally
his own family joined the caravans of people
forced to abandon ancestral lands

so in his new home far across a sea of grief
the boy joined a team, and sent every ball
rocketing, until coaches began to call him
a bonus baby who could someday go pro
and receive millions for signing a contract
but money was never the boy's goal
all he needed was freedom
to dream

MASCULINIDADES
Vida

In 2022, a Cuban photographer named Monik Molinet
tweeted pictures of various men wearing flowers
behind their ears as a pledge of nonviolence
toward women.

Five million people reacted immediately—nearly half
the island's entire population—but to my dismay
many of them called Molinet's peaceful photos
an attack against the dignity
of men.

MASCULINIDADES
Adán

Vida shows me those photos of muscular guys
with a single blossom or a whole bouquet
arranged behind one ear—white, red, pink,
or purple flowers above beards, stubble,
mustaches, frowns, grins, delighted smiles,
each man dedicated to the delicacy of petals
as a promise of kindness
that makes us strong
not weak.

ALMOST EIGHTEEN
Adán

Tomorrow it will feel strange to suddenly
be considered an adult.

I struggled when we first arrived from Cuba.
I had to learn English, so at school I was silent
while slamming a bat into a ball
became
my
own
private
language
of rage.

Today my acceptance letter arrived—University of Miami,
the Hurricanes, a full baseball scholarship, pediatric
sports therapy major, so I can help kids like my sister
who doesn't need a wheelchair when she exercises
to strengthen her courage along with her muscles.
If a pro team offer comes through, I don't know
whether I'll accept or stick with this college plan.
Why does the future have to be so confusing?

ADMISSIONS LETTER
Vida

Florida International University
double major, photography and zoology
until I decide whether I'm patient enough
for grad school in wildlife biology
or veterinary medicine.
Either way
I'm ready
to celebrate!

My first real date with Adán will be a visit
to an old-fashioned candy store, so our memories
can overflow with the scent and flavor of childhood.

Excitement tumbles around in my mind
like a pebble in water, edges polished
by waves
on an island's
shore.

MEMORIES OF THE
CHOCOLATE FOREST
Vida and Adán

Our familias worked together on a collective farm
in el monte, slicing big, ripe cacao pods
away from the trees.

With machetes, adults cracked the sun-hued pods,
removed pulpy seeds, arranged them on green
banana leaves in a fermentation box, turned the beans
over and over for several days, then dried them on tarps,
evenly spaced so light could reach every side, no clumps
where mold might grow and spoil the flavor.

Roast, winnow, grind, taste—bitter!
Boil with sugar, honey, coffee, or spices.
Our parents learned fancy ways to refine,
temper, conch, and flavor the chocolate
until it met demanding standards
for Swiss and Belgian investors
who promised to market
our delicious chocolate truffles
overseas, but that was before
drought and floods
murdered the trees

leaving hungry birds
and creatures
including
human
refugees.

Now
the only way
to taste and smell
our forested childhood
is inside this candy store
with our eyes
closed.

OPEN
Vida

In the chocolate forest
everyone believed that cacao
is a heart-opener
capable of stimulating
blood flow, to help us learn,
understand, thrive,
and grow.

I don't know if those old legends are true
but I'm beginning to feel certain that my own
fiery red corazón
is already
unfolding
like a letter
in a bottle
after a long
journey
across
blue
sea.

AGE
Adán

Reminiscing as we taste chocolate
eyes
closed
hands
clasped
memories
wide-open.

The night is long
fragrant
sweet.

We don't need to rush
any decisions
beyond
kissing.

Tomorrow I'll be eighteen.
Adult dilemmas will arrive soon enough.

CELEBRATION
Vida

On Adán's eighteenth birthday
Luci, Graciela, and Libertad ask me to host
a surprise party for their brother, at my house.

I'm nervous, because Abuelita
has just arrived home from Borneo,
where she photographed orphaned orangutans
in a devastated landscape
of deforestation . . .

but she's wiped her tears, and now she's excited
about meeting my new novio.

Adán's sisters style my hair, paint my nails,
and talk me into wearing a midnight-blue dress
that reveals too much cleavage.

Will his parents and abuelos hate me
if the first time I meet them
I look
sexy?

DREAMS OF ADULTHOOD
Vida

in just a few weeks
I'll be eighteen too,
an age of big choices
with freedom to make
huge decisions, maybe
I'll break the old frame
and seek new ways to

escape

SOBER AT EIGHTEEN
Adán

I'm wary of any situation
that puts Papi and Abuelo
in the same room with me
while they're drunk.

I tuck a coral-hued hibiscus
behind one ear, as a gesture
of masculinidad without fear.

At first everything seems comfortable,
my family, coach, and teammates
all laughing at jokes told in Spanglish
and making fun of me
for looking floral.

Vida doesn't mock me.
I wish we were alone.

Instead, we have to keep chatting
with each other's friends, pretending
we're satisfied with conversations
at a moment when I'd rather be
stargazing

or beachcombing
anything natural
and quiet
outdoors
with the most beautiful girl
on the whole flowery globe.

DANCE
Vida

relaxed in your arms
it's easy to imagine
a world of our own

when the children danced in midair
they sensed solid land far below

both their swift aerial escape
and the slow return to Earth
were wondrous . . .

but wonders vanish
in the presence of doubt
so they never questioned
magic
faith
or flight

ALARMED
Adán

Abuelo starts wandering
from room to room, a scowl on his face
as he recognizes the signature
on Rita's photographs.

Her pictures are stunning.
Girls in Mexico run races in skirts and sandals,
a child on a cliff in Nepal harvests wild honey,
fishermen, feasts, riots, hunger, a farmer
on horseback, the ruins of our houses
in Cuba, dead cacao trees,
the dried-up
waterfall.

A jacana bird with long toes
walks on the surface of a pond—miraculous—
but my grandfather's horrified expression
warns me that just like so many other
cubanos en Miami, he will never accept
any exile who returns to the island
after fleeing.

EXPOSED
Vida

I didn't think about the stack of new,
unframed photos from Rita's most recent
incognito trip to Cuba, when she sneaked in
with a tourist visa, even though she's really
an exiled dissident, her journalism forbidden.

The photos show food lines that stretch
for blocks, and the faces of people who finally reach
their turn, only to discover that all the rationed
daily bread is gone.

There are pictures of crumbling schools
and abandoned hospitals beside new hotels
with luxury spas, and medical clinics for tourists.

If I'd warned Adán, we could have hidden this evidence
of my grandmother's investigative travel,
with all its twisted
ways of being perceived in Florida, where so many exiles
hate anyone who returns to the island,
because they assume
all travelers must spend money that benefits
the corrupt dictatorship.

But I know my abuelita,
she stays with friends and relatives
I've never met, instead of paying for hotels owned
by the government, and I can't help feeling grateful
because if she didn't keep visiting la isla,
she would never have been able
to rescue me
from the edge
of death.

Now, as Adán's abuelo glares
at the photos of our birthplace
his shocked expression shifts
into a flaming rage
that I can only describe
as murderous.

DREAD
Adán

The moment
when our grandparents
recognize each other
is like a hurricane warning
ominous
dark
suffocating.

The breath of everyone in this room
suddenly feels vulnerable
to a rapidly plummeting
loss
of
air.

Can people actually die
of terror?

UPROAR
Adán

Abuelo starts yelling,
he calls Rita a puta, and then
to my horror, he shoves her
as if she were a man
in a bar
drunk
and stumbling
just like him.

I can't let him push an old woman
so I grab his wrists, knowing that I risk
becoming the target of his fists.

Papi, Abuela, Mami, and my sisters
all form a circle around us, forcing me
to move my grandpa toward the door
outside
away
from
disaster.

SHOCK
Vida

Everyone leaves.
Only Rita and I remain
surrounded by her photos
and my tangible waves
of disbelief.

How can anyone attack someone
just for traveling back to our homeland?

There must be another layer of hatred
some resentment that was carried
across the sea
long ago.

I feel like I'm standing   on a crumbling bridge
unable to reach   either shore.

DIVIDING LINES
Adán

We've crossed
            into a hostile territory
with imaginary borders

an inherited
            horizon
of sorrow

no one in my family speaks
about anything that happened
before my birth

so there's no way to find out
why Abuelo detests
my girlfriend's abuela
so deeply.

At home, the entire family falls silent
as if we're mourning at a funeral
that has nothing to do with death.

CONFESSION
Vida

Shaking
with emotion
Rita sits beside me
clutches my hands
and tells me the story
of her youth in el monte
where she wrote articles
for a prohibited newsletter
that revealed all the secrets
of government corruption.

Supplies stolen from hospitals
were diverted to hotels for tourists.

Dengue epidemics were kept secret
to avoid frightening foreigners.

Doctors who broke the silence
were arrested and lost their licenses.

Neighbors caught reading
the banned information
were arrested on charges

of possessing enemy propaganda
even though the facts were completely true.

Adán's abuelo was one of the readers
punished for craving honest news.

Rita was arrested too, but after a year
she was released and exiled to Spain
where she became famous.

Later, in Miami, she found a loyal audience
for dramatic pictures that tell complex stories
without words.

She doesn't expect anyone to forgive her
for that early work, the articles that resulted
in suffering, instead of government reform.

She promises she'll try to apologize
if she ever has a chance to talk
and be heard.

I NEVER KNEW . . .
Adán

that Abuelo was sent to a forced labor camp
for the crime of reading an illegal newspaper
or that he still blames Rita after thirty years,
and there's no way I could have guessed
that my grandfather would now order me
to stay away from Vida
as if I'm a modern Romeo
caught in the middle
of some ancient rivalry
that has nothing to do
with Julieta
or love.

the children
often noticed
rays of hatred
that flashed
back and forth
between adults

but creatures
need heroes
so the children
ignored grown-ups
while they invented their own
serene island of kindness
within the adults'
turbulent
archipelago
of fury
and fear

LEGACY

Adán

By the end of that catastrophic surprise party
Vida looked so sad that her midnight dress
and forest-green eyes
made her seem as lonely
as a girl in a story about orphans.

Now I'm officially an adult
but I've inherited chaos.

Everything seems so confusing
that I spend the next morning alone
at a batting cage
slamming
the ball
with all
my force.

I should have tried to see Vida sooner
because now, when I go home to change
my clothes, I discover another
catastrophe.

EMERGENCY

Adán

Abuelo's fist
clutches his chest.

Sirens.
Ambulance.
Anguish.

No phones are allowed in the cardiac wing
of the hospital, so I can't call Vida
or check for texts.

Intensive care only permits one visitor at a time.
I wait my turn, after Abuela, Papi, Mami,
and all three sisters, but by then
my grandfather is awake
and he refuses to see me unless I promise
to break up with the only girl I've ever loved.

I feel like a bird
in a cage
tortured.

GHOSTED
Vida

puzzle pieces
        crumble
    as I struggle to find lost   hope

you hover

                beyond reach

while I feel
      like
        a train
          on the
            way
              to

                nowhere
zigzags
      hairpin turns
volcanic peaks
      tunnels

                darkness

somewhere far away
love wanders   abandoned

TRUTH AND DESPAIR
Adán

at home I strive to float
above all the adult arguments
but there's no way to lift
                my imagination

only love is strong enough
              for levitation

and I haven't spoken to Vida—I know
I'm a bestia if I don't call her, but so soon
after Abuelo's open-heart surgery
who knows what will happen to him
if he rages

either way
I'm a beast

DESOLATE

Vida

alone
alone
alone

barely aware
of feeling alive

oh, how I long to visit
a pet shelter, adopt a kitten or puppy
to make up for the loss of love
an illusion that so swiftly
slipped away

but soon summer will arrive
I'll have a job and no one will be home
so my sorrowful dog or cat would be

alone
alone
alone

FEMINISTish MEN AND SILENCED WOMEN
Vida

One flower
draped over your ear
won't be enough to help you listen
and hear all the things I won't know
how to say if I ever trust you enough
to speak.

LOST AND NEVER FOUND
Adán

If only *love* and *hope* were synonyms.
The scent of a blossom could become truth.

If only I never had to choose
between ancestors
and you.

FROM LIGHT TO LIGHT
Vida

I need an instruction manual
for living in a world where angry old men
still shove women and call them putas,
a world where young men say they're in love
and then vanish.

So I read *We Should All Be Feminists*
by Chimamanda Ngozi Adichie, and then I find
a poem by Reina María Rodríguez, who describes islands
as imaginary worlds inside ourselves,
and a verse by Excilia Saldaña,
who describes wings as islands
and islands as wings.

When I try to make sense of my own feelings
confusion leads me back to the lens of a camera
where I seize the radiant glow of golden hours
that absorb shadows from the sun
every evening, as if Earth only sees
her own beauty
in twilight.

DANCING WITH ANIMALS
Vida

so alone
while Rita travels
and Adán avoids me
I read and croon in a howling voice
to owls, mockingbirds, and warblers
at the serene wildlife sanctuary
where I dance
with an orphaned bobcat
as both of us struggle
to figure out
where
we belong
in life's challenging hierarchy
of kingdom, phylum, class, order,
family, genus, species,
voice,
rhythm,
song

ALL MY OWN VERSES ARE SHORT TODAY
Vida

islands
within islands
wordless

the only creatures
the children could never rescue
were fighting cocks
worn like ornaments
on the shoulders
of gamblers

wild pigs
hunted for meat

rooftop dogs
chained for guard duty
no ladder in sight

government-owned cattle
herded by soldiers

horses rented to tourists
constantly accompanied by guides

and hundreds of endangered species
held captive at a zoo in the city, where cages
were their only chance to survive
for a few more days or years

LOST LOVE PALINDROME
Vida

I scribble words, lift my camera,
transform syllables into pictures:

island	beneath	sea	beneath	island
love	above	clouds	above	love
past	hidden	now	hidden	past

BROKEN HEART SYNDROME
Vida

The veterinarian at the wildlife sanctuary tells me
that whenever an African wild dog
is separated from her pack
she dies of loneliness, so zoo vets
bring at least two close companions
into the clinic, like visitors in a hospital
patiently awaiting miracles.

I miss the book club.
Now, instead of friends,
I have photos and poems,
owls, hawks, and bobcats,
along with my own
constantly changing
spontaneous songs
each lyric an arrow
in wild air, piercing
my own
desperate
breath.

REALITY
Adán

I feel numb from the hasty decision
to dump my novia, at least until Abuelo
recovers from open-heart surgery.

They cracked his chest.
Plunged past bones.
Excavated el corazón.

But Luci says if I want to be a genuine feminist,
I need to listen to all my sisters, who see Rita
as a hero, risking her life every time
she travels to photograph injustice.

In theory, I agree, but realistically
I'll never be able to forgive myself
if my grandfather dies of rage
simply because I refused to obey
his warning to stay away
from love.

JOB OFFER
Adán

I'd forgotten that I even applied!
Abuelo is better now, but he can't work,
so he's home all the time, and I can't wait
to escape, so as soon as I accept the Zoo Camp job,
everything feels a bit more hopeful.
Next week is graduation,
then this job, and in the fall,
either college
or a pro team . . .

I pick up my phone,
wishing I could share this news
with Vida, but I know she wouldn't
believe me, even if I apologized
for all the ghosting
of her calls
and texts.

There's nothing to do but celebrate alone
at the batting cages, pretending she still
loves me.

LA MEMORIA DEL AMOR
Vida

The memory of love
is an empty house and hollow heart
but not forever, because
minds are winged islands
        so I try
           to make my thoughts   fly

but it takes two minds to levitate
and like migratory birds
my invisible wishes
keep returning
to this nest
of emptiness.

GRADUATION
Adán

cap
gown
speeches

diploma
teammates
coach

padres
hermanas
abuelos

if only I felt as festive
as everyone else expects

all I have from you is one text
that says you won't listen
to my apology
not yet

HIGH SCHOOL DIPLOMA
Vida

No graduation ceremony
just a sheet of white paper
sprinkled with black ink
waiting for me
in the mailbox.

Meanwhile, all over the wildlife sanctuary
birds, mammals, and reptiles congratulate me
by listening to my wordless new songs, tapped out
with the rhythm of feet and wings
as I dance
never alone
always accompanied
by other survivors, wounded creatures
who instinctively understand movement
and music.

the girl's voice
was a powerful force
that could heal any timid
creature's
fear

one lyrical song
was enough to lift the spirits
of a weary ox or horse
as if the rhymed lyrics
were feathers

ARRIVAL
Adán

My first day of summer work
is such a relief that even though it's just
going to be training all week, I feel proud
of the slightly weird uniform—Zoo Camp hat,
bright green shirt, khaki shorts, hiking boots,
and a flamingo-pink name tag
that proclaims *Adán Palmero*
Assistant Counselor.

I wish Luci could be one of the kids
at this camp, but she needs summer school
to bring her grades up.

I've tried to see Vida a thousand times
but she keeps refusing to open her door
so now, when I see her right inside
the zoo entrance, I feel
like she might be imaginary
and this is just my own

wind-borne vision.

GRACEFUL
Vida

My name tag says *Vida Serena Sierra*
Assistant Counselor.

I hope it's official enough to allow me
to cross this low barrier and enter the dance
of fifty flamingos
as they march
in a rhythmic
procession
pink
legs
wings
beaks
turn
swirl
twirl
spin
with synchrony
as if they've rehearsed
our flightless
ballet.

THE AFFECTION OF FLAMINGOS
Vida

Their wings are clipped.
No escape.
So they embrace my friendship
as if I were a familiar animal keeper
who they dance with every day.

I'm so glad this is a breeding facility
that consists entirely of huge natural habitats
instead of one of those places for tourists
with thousands of species
trapped in small cages.

Caribbean flamingos aren't endangered yet
but they live on shorelines, so rising sea levels
will eventually threaten their colonies.
In the meantime
at least they have me
to love them.

CRÈCHE
Vida

I
watch
a flamingo father
as he sings to a single
large egg, tucked into
a volcano-shaped nest
made of crumbling, sandy mud
the color of a shadowy sunset.

Humans should learn from birds who know
that parental voices can be so clearly heard
from deep inside the secret world
of a fragile
shell.

Both parents feed flamingo milk to the hatchlings,
a creamy mixture of their own food, transformed
into a pink smoothie, then regurgitated
and shared.

SCENT IS A MEMORY
Vida

Caribbean flamingos
are strong island creatures—
five feet tall with a five-foot wingspan.

They can fly thirty-five miles per hour
   hundreds of miles per day
    unless they live in a zoo
feathers clipped
or even amputated.

Beaks filter water and mud through threadlike combs
that sift edible crustaceans, insects, and algae,
the carotene a pigment that turns the birds pink.

Their crèche smells like mud, this petrichor aroma
of wet soil after rain, a fragrance that reminds me
of Cuba
but also of dengue fever—I'm so glad I remembered
to smear my arms, legs, and face with the foul odor
of insect repellant.

FLIGHTLESS
Adán

You look different—braided hair
and a frown that's clearly directed at me
as you dart away, pink birds scattering
in every direction.

If only you would stay and hear
my endless apologies, the words so small
for a mistake of such magnitude.

I can't blame you.
If I were the ghosted one
I would flee too.

ZOO JOB ORIENTATION
Vida

I can't believe
we ended up working together!
In the room where counselors meet
for training, I sit as far away from you as possible.
My veins twitch like electric wires.
My skin feels reptilian, so tight and raw
that it might shed, leaving me unprotected
while my skull splits open to release a flood
of sorrow or rage—at this point it's impossible
to tell the difference.

Your hair is short.
Baseball season must be over.
I liked it better when it was shaggy
and you believed
in the magic
of luck.

Maybe working with animals
will help both of us understand
the strange brains of humans.

PREPAREDNESS
Adán

You refuse to make eye contact, but just being
in the same room makes me struggle
to concentrate on instructions
for emergencies.

If anyone falls into a predator's enclosure . . .
If a child tries to steal a rare bird's feather . . .
If someone gets sick . . .
If a fire breaks out . . .
If a hurricane is approaching . . .
Fights between rival male creatures . . .
Fights between tourists or students . . .
Inappropriate behavior, language, gestures . . .
Combative parents?
Bomb threats?
Active shooters?
I don't get it.
Why would anyone come to a zoo
acting more ferocious than the tigers?

DISASTER PLAN
Vida

We have to practice
hurricane preparedness.
It strikes me as surrealistic
but zoos are rarely evacuated
because moving is so traumatic
that the risk of heart failure is greater
than danger from rainfall and wind,
so when a storm is getting close
signs and tarps will be taken down,
meals are prepared in advance,
cleaning supplies, generators,
fuel, cots, blankets for a crew
of brave zookeepers
who are willing
to stay
and risk
death.

WISTFUL AND HOPEFUL
Vida

After all the strange information
I try to absorb during training
comes a painful experience
that I hadn't imagined.

Children walk up to me holding the hands
of their parents, and suddenly I feel newly
orphaned
all over
again
and
again.

At least the head counselor is older, calm
and confident, her Haitian accent musical
as she tells me her name is Islande.

Together, she proclaims,
you and I will show all these city kids
how to love nature.

all the cacao trees were dying
from a leaf rust fungus that spread
like fire, vultures circling overhead
waiting to eat any creature
that starved

but each horse or parrot
the boy rescued from strangers
was fed and hugged by the girl
whose youthful parents rejoiced
along with the children

poverty was never enough
to make survival
seem impossible

grateful animals
brought enough beauty
to make every moment hopeful

YOUNG NATURALISTS
Adán

Teenagers.
Thirteen to sixteen years old.
I'm so glad I ended up as an assistant
instead of a lead counselor, because this job
won't be easy—the campers are already
scrolling their phones, instead of listening
or asking questions.

Physiology, animal behavior, biodiversity,
there's so much I need to learn so I can teach.

My boss is a college kid called Chet
who glances over at Vida and nods at her,
but she ignores him, so he smirks and tells me
he knew her when they were both Zooies
at a boarding school.

I can't read her subtle expressions like I used to
when we were close, so it's impossible to know
whether she hates both of us, or does she just
detest me?

ZOO MUSIC
Vida

Voices from each habitat,
songs in the languages of animals,
odors from distant forests,
memories of racing to escape
an attack by humans—the world's
most dangerous creatures—and now
I have to work so close to both men,
the guy who just broke my heart,
and a witness of the crime
that almost destroyed me . . .

but the music of zoo voices grows
and echoes
light-years between the shy girl
I used to be
and this grown woman emerging
with a burst of fury.

If either one of them tries to touch me,
I'll screech, shriek, scream!

WE
Vida

With Chet right in front of me
I feel as if I'm being hunted again,
so I finally decide to ask for guidance
from every adult female I know.
Rita, Graciela, Libertad, even Islande
despite her role as my boss.
They all say the same thing.
We need a good lawyer.
We'll tell HR and the boarding school
that Chet refused to admit he saw exactly
what happened, and that's why I did not dare
to bring charges, because it would have turned into
he said, she said, instead of
me too.

The way grown women say "we" instead of "you"
helps me feel brave and strong.
No girl should ever have to shout
about injustice
alone.

AGILITY
Adán

I don't know what's going on
and Vida won't speak to me
so I concentrate on learning
how to teach, using trained
animal ambassadors
for our first few lessons.

Chet shows me how to toss a lure
high above the head of a serval
an African wildcat who leaps
vertically
to seize
fake
prey
as if it were a real bird
in bright sky
soaring!

Baseball players could learn from servals
and cheetahs, and every other swift
species of feline.

THE CHEETAH RUN
Vida

All the paperwork has been filed
by a lawyer Rita hired.

Now it's a waiting game
while I help Islande release
a sleek Rhodesian Ridgeback dog
trained to run after a fake rabbit
pulled on a string.

As soon as the canine race is over
a cheetah follows with astonishing speed
and then the two swift creatures relax
and play together.

Both were orphans
raised as siblings.

As we watch them, the children and I
coo like doves, touched by the sight
of such an unusual interspecies friendship.

ZOOCHOSIS
Adán

Chet and I teach campers how to create
enrichment activities to help animals
who are bored
in small enclosures.

Fruit-filled piñatas for elephants.
Bone-and-blood puzzles for lions.
Fish inside ice cubes for a polar bear
whose exhibit is exactly one millionth
of the size of her natural territory
in the wild.

Sometimes I feel just as trapped
as these creatures, as if I've never really
experienced my true
emotional habitat.

I feel so much smaller
than when Vida
loved me.

THE WAITING GAME
Vida

While I wait for life to eventually make sense
I help Islande teach small children how to stroke
a hedgehog—head to tail, never the reverse.

We offer treats to a young rhino
by poking a carrot through a sturdy fence,
and we feed romaine lettuce to giraffes
by standing on an elevated platform
as we admire their long blue tongues
and enormous eyes.

We create a leafy birthday cake
for a ten-year-old orangutan, and meat pies
for a five-year-old Siberian tiger, and I don't
tell anyone that next week I'll be eighteen
because the last thing I need right now
is for Adán to be sweet to me
for only one
day.

on the girl's seventh birthday
all she wanted to do was drift
between wishes
as she waited
for the boy
to bring
a cake of fragrant
homegrown chocolate
each cacao seed pounded
and sweetened so easily
in a forest where closeness
had not yet become
an impossible
daydream

SECRECY
Adán

At home
my sisters
whisper.

At work
Islande glares
at Chet.

If I knew what was going on,
I might be able to have an opinion,
but when everyone else keeps secrets
all I can do
is reveal
my own.

I need to really apologize, explain, and hope Vida
eventually forgives me for obeying Abuelo
when he ordered me
to dump her.

BEE FENCE
Adán

I don't know why I keep procrastinating
instead of speaking to Vida, and letting her
sting me with her anger.

Teaching other teens feels both intimidating
and worthwhile.

We learn about the fear elephants experience
in the presence of tiny bees.

Hives make a stronger barrier than chain link
or electricity.

Maybe that's why I need to separate myself
from family violence.

Just tiny wings in air, buzzing
to warn Papi and Abuelo that they'd better not
cross into my personal territory
of peace.

BELL SONG
Vida

Teaching children is a maze
of joy and wonder!

We help train an enormous tortoise
to follow the trail made by clanging a cowbell
while rustling a tempting feast of edible leaves
that lead to safety inside a concrete and steel
night house, protection against storms
on this peninsula
of hurricanes.

We train other animals too.
Raisins are the best way to tempt and lead
wallabies, lemurs love fresh grapes, gorillas
respond to oats with honey,
rhinos follow alfalfa,
otters can't resist crab meat,
orangutans crave toasted pumpkin seeds,
and to move a grizzly bear, no treat is more effective
than strawberry jam.

MULTIPLICATION FROM ADDITION
Adán

Teaching Zoo Camp is sorrowful
when I have to explain that there are only
twenty
red wolves
alive
in the wild.

I stand reverently, watching two
of the last two hundred survivors
held captive
in breeding zoos.

I feel like I'm riding Noah's ark
on dry land.

At least there's a chance that two
plus two hundred
can eventually
become twenty thousand.

ZOO PHOTOGRAPHY
Vida

My camera mourns the solitude
of a widowed Cuban parrot
in love with his own reflection
in a mirror.

My lens rejoices along with a rhino
who scrubs her itchy head against
a rolling brush donated by a car wash.

Both the camera and the rhino
are so relieved by survival—this last female
of her species now pregnant
with artificially inseminated sperm
flown here from a male survivor in a distant land.

Fortunately, the laughter of children is a gift
that travels from one human to another, as babies
of a thousand species all over the breeding zoo
romp, race, leap, and pose for photos
that give me hope
for the future.

PERCUSSION
Vida

Behind the camera, my eye celebrates
the drumming of flamingo feet against mud
while my heart pounds whenever you
are nearby.

Wild flamingos often join the captives
with their clipped wings, making me wonder
if zoo birds can understand the risks
and possibilities
of wildness.

Do they envy
birds who fly?

Will I ever be able to touch you again
and remember the freedom
of kisses?

FINALLY
Adán

Vida comes to me with a problem to solve.
The flamingo nests aren't sturdy enough,
this mud is too sandy, so soft that it crumbles.

She asks me to find a source of baseball stadium
red clay, thick and sticky, as if we are planning
to open a ceramic studio.

Of course I say yes—all it takes is a phone call
to Coach, who knows everyone in the sport.

Vida's smile
is my Hall of Fame
prize.

Now if only she would speak to me
about our own future, instead of
the love life of birds.

MELANCHOLY BIRTHDAY
Vida

Abuelita was supposed to be home with me
but her flight was delayed, so I spend Saturday
at the wildlife sanctuary, sharing cupcakes
with Dr. Ramos, the veterinarian.

When she leaves, I'm alone with owls
who might never fly again
after being shot by men
who see them as evil omens.

Each creature in this refuge
has suffered because of humans
but while they're here, they trust me,
so I sing old Cuban love songs
as if I still believed in the fantasy
of el amor and happy
ever after.

TURMOIL
Adán

I stand outside the wildlife sanctuary
listening to your voice as you serenade
wounded animals.

Your lyrics can't reach me
through this locked door
so I knock and pound
rhythmically
as if drumming
until finally
you face me
and listen
to my plea.

I know I should have explained right away.
Now my heart has turned
      into a cyclone
           always whirling
       never peaceful
as I apologize
over and over . . .

FORGIVENESS?
Vida

divided pathways
my emotions still frozen
by those ghostly
days of coldness
so
ice
is all
I can offer

until you reach
take my hands
and apologize so fervently
that I almost believe you
but when I strive to answer
my words feel inadequate

I imagine
just one embrace
a simple kiss
         then levitation
            wild space   wide-open
but that's not enough
yet

HOW TO FORGIVE
Vida

Somehow
I need to remove
the question mark
from my mind
convince myself
that pain won't be
repeated.

That
seems
impossible
but so does
love.

The border between past and future
is now, so I hurl myself into the present
and force my hurt and fears away
back where they belong
before
and
after
today.

AFTER FORGIVENESS
Vida

love is a poem
a state of being
house
land
river
canoe
origin story
sacred mountain
scent of chocolate
waterfall
love
     is a song
a doorway
     illuminated
light of your eyes
     circle of words
our spiral
     embrace
this second chance
         miraculous

TIMEKEEPER
Vida

Is there really an age
when somehow
I will
stop
counting
kisses?

LIFE FLOATS . . .
Adán

in a way that never makes sense
but right now all my senses are alive
sight of you scent of you sound taste touch

pigeons hear the approach of distant earthquakes
elephants smell water from twelve miles away

together you and I detect an invisible mist
of possibilities, the same way flowers contain
hidden pigments, shimmering colors
that only hummingbirds
can see

LIFE GLIDES . . .
Vida

while our natural habitat of midair flight grows
from the poetry of closeness, where somehow
love
rhymes
with *freedom*

LIFE RING TATTOO
Adán

The next morning feels like forever
so I wrap your name around my finger
　　　　　V　　　　　　A
　　　　　　I　　D

a
whorl
　　　that rises　　　from mind　　　to sky
then back
to Earth
a flight
through
my heart

on a sunlit day
in aromatic mountains
during a lull between disasters
the girl asked the boy to marry her
someday

so he painted a ring
on his finger
with ink

and she made her own anillo
from a green leaf
pretending it was smooth stone
soothing jade
like the artifacts they often
discovered
in caves hidden behind waterfalls
stone carved with sky designs
left behind
by ancestors

SOOTHING JADE
Vida

so many years after I gave you a leafy anillo
you
drop
to
one
knee
and offer me a stone ring
deep green like herbs, ferns, trees
breath
from forested
growth

now
we'll be inseparable
just like we imagined
when we were only seven
and forever was a legend
from our ancestral
future

LIFE SPAN
Vida

flamingos live thirty years
in captivity
or sixty in a zoo

humans have only a few decades
to feel trapped or free
but hope soars between you
and me
rippling like music
or fragrance
the wavy
flow
of time

AVIARY OF THE HEART
Adán

love
    is
       a
          feather

and a wing

and
   all
      the
        air
in between

love is the nest
we return to after
          each   flight

ZOO CAMP SCHEDULE
Vida

Every few days there's a new group
of young children, so I never really have a chance
to learn names, I just read the tags on green vests
that make little kids easy to find in a crowd
of Adán's class, the elusive teens who keep
slipping away
to flirt.

ZOO CAMP PURPOSE
Adán

Education.
Conservation.
Attention.
Wonder.

It all sounds so impossible to communicate
to teens who are just a few years younger than me,
but they need optimism—
without it, there's only
apathy.

FOREVER MEETS NOW
Vida

Heat and rain make each day
a guessing game, indoors or outside,
hurricane warning or tropical storm?

Everything changes constantly, so all I can do
is feel joyful in this moment when I'm with you
surrounded by manatees, iguanas, jutías,
Cuban crocodiles, and other rare
island creatures.

I photograph animals
who embrace each other
with long necks
or coiled tails
instead of arms.

I try to answer children's questions
about the climate crisis, endangered species,
and ways to help animals survive, survive, survive . . .

PLOT TWIST
Adán

My sisters invite me
to a book club meeting at Rita's house
and even though Luci is still so young
we discuss *Speak* by Laurie Halse Anderson,
and then we talk about Chet, whose role
in the shocking attack against Vida
is clear now—a lawyer and Islande
got him to confess
that he was a lookout
not a witness.

His job at the zoo is over, but Vida still begs me
to promise that if we ever cross paths again, I won't
beat him up, because she doesn't want to visit me
in prison, if I get arrested
for assault
with a baseball bat . . .

so even though words feel like fists
in my throat, I choke them out—I promise
to be patient, and wait for justice.

JUBILATION
Vida

Now that she knows about Chet
and the boarding school attack
Rita decides to retire, but in Spanish
retiring from a job is jubilarse, and *jubilation*
describes my own feelings right now.

I'm officially retiring from my guilt
about not speaking up sooner.

Imagine how many girls might be spared fear and pain
if we manage to get attempted rapists arrested right away
instead of waiting until it's almost too late.

My lawyer is already busy collecting
testimonies from other violated students.
I wasn't the only one, that much is clearly
a shared truth, and if we are all heard
in a courtroom, our voices will be
more powerful
than muscles.

NO MORE EUPHEMISMS
Vida

Newsmen say *molest* instead of *rape*
misinformation in place of lies
allegations instead of events.

I imagine the reason
is Chet's family's wealth.
Influence is respected
more than facts.

But I'm through with euphemistic
substitutions for truth.

I need to face life's ugliness
with words that embarrass me
even though they should only
be shameful
to the perpetrators.

NO MORE PABLO NERUDA LOVE POEMS
Vida

Our book club decides to boycott a man
who received a Nobel Prize, despite bragging
about rape.

Neruda boasted in his memoir
that when he attacked his Tamil maid in Ceylon
he viewed her as inhuman
a motionless statue
of stone.

Now I'm turning his memory into dust
the love poems I used to enjoy so much
blown away by wind from herstory's
shouting voice.

BONOBOS
Adán

If only men were less aggressive.
Chimpanzees patrol territorial borders
but their close relatives the bonobos
are friendly to strangers.

Bonobos never kill each other,
and when a male wants to mate
he has to be polite enough
to receive the approval
of the female's mother.

Bonobos are so far ahead of humans
in the interspecies evolution
of gentleness.

WORD SEARCH
Vida

With Chet fired from his zoo job,
Islande helps Adán teach the teen group
while I handle younger kids on my own.

We prepare scavenger hunts for anteaters,
create edible piñatas for grizzly bears,
laugh as a baby eland frolics,
and marvel at the surprisingly
powerful roar
of a cute
little
koala.

I feel like I'm inside a crossword puzzle,
searching for synonyms big enough
to communicate my full range
of rage
and hope.

PATROLLING LOVE'S BORDERS
Vida

I'm glad Islande is in charge of the teens
because her air of authority helps curb
the flirtatious behavior of girls
who so obviously have crushes
on my boyfriend.

Until now
I never knew
that I would be
the jealous type
fiercely territorial
like a prowling
creature.

When I tell Adán, he looks surprised
and says he would feel the same way.

Maybe we both need to learn
how to trust each other
completely.

the climate changed so abruptly
that even wise adults were baffled
and only the children
never
lost hope

creatures
could adapt
couldn't they?

illusions of safety
were almost as comforting
as imaginary dances in midair

all it takes is levitation
to make stormy clouds seem
less dangerous

BIODIVERSITY
Adán

Each afternoon, we study the subjects we'll teach
the next morning, about global conservation projects
that coordinate plans for breeding rare species
all over the world.

Some of the babies raised here will eventually
be released in their natural habitats, but others
have to stay until poachers and logging
and climate catastrophes
are somehow controlled.

It's hard to convince teenagers to feel hopeful
but it's easy to show them how to prepare meals
for giant otters, capybaras, emus, condors,
and golden lion tamarins
with fur like sunlight
and eyes that radiate
rainforest
secrets.

ZOO ARK
Vida

wonderstruck children
in a world of rare creatures
waiting for mercy

INTERSPECIES KINSHIP
Vida

I have permission to arrive early
and stay late, throughout the two
golden hours—just after dawn
and right before dusk.
My photos of endangered animals at the zoo
are inferior to professional images
yet still able to inspire children
as they learn to see creatures
as kin, worthy of kindness

f   f
r   u
a   t
m   u
e   r
d   e

    shared

EXHIBIT IN MY MIND
Vida

I imagine which pictures I'll frame
if Islande succeeds in her request
for an exhibit of my photos!

The one of a jaguar walking across
her own reflection in a stream,
an owl at the moment of his release
after his wings have healed and he
can once again fly free, a flamingo
with the sunrise behind her head
so she resembles a pink angel
with a golden halo.
A baby tree kangaroo
peering from his mother's pouch.
A great blue heron perched behind a white egret
so they appear to be each other's shadow.

A close-up of you
my smile reflected
in your eye.

COMMUNICATION
Vida

We're the only animals with a white sclera
surrounding the colorful iris of the eye.

That's how we see each other's emotions
and reveal our own feelings so clearly
    the direction
        of a gaze
            easy to follow.

When the entire eye is dark, animals watch
each other's gestures and movements
instead of expressions.

While I explain this to young children
they test my theory, creating drawings
of each other
with impenetrable
stares.

cliff
dive
the
boy
and
girl
leaped
fingers
and gazes
swooping
together

forever
a visible
pool
of
joy

NIGHT ZOO
Vida

Once each month
there's an overnight camp
with storytellers from all over the world
and guest speakers, like the young couple
named Leandro and Ana, who bring a blue
conservation dog called Cielo,
trained to help scientists
find pumas in California
and panthers in Florida.

When Leandro says Cielo is a Cuban singing dog
I remember old stories about their serenades
and matchmaking skills, both so legendary
that now I feel like we're in a fairy tale
with love at the center of time flow's
past-present-future
all linked by echoes
of high-flying
light-filled
island
voices.

CANINE DAYDREAM
Adán

Vida and I decide
to adopt our own dog
from a shelter, after the end of summer
when we'll both be starting college
with a bit of free time on weekends,
ready to train a conservation canine
who can detect the scent
of any rare animal
that needs to be
studied
or rescued.

Our conversation about noses and odors
reminds us that we both smell like creatures
ourselves, these zoo uniforms constantly
stained with the food, urine, fur, and feces
of one endangered species or another.

Inside our minds, it's the fragrance
of a rewilding daydream.

NOCTURNAL
Vida

Luci, Graciela, and Libertad
join us for the Night Zoo Sleepover Camp
where they're free to explore all evening,
while our job
is guarding animals
to make sure people
don't climb fences,
throw litter,
or try to feed
creatures.

Awake all night
we listen to snarls,
howls, whistles,
and growls, while campers
stretch out in sleeping bags
feeling safe, because they imagine
that we are there to protect
humans.

SO CLOSE
Adán

nocturnal
together

my mind
feels like mist

a waterfall
of emotions

our hands
    twine
        so tightly

as we stand
    side by side
        minds   adrift

DAWN
Vida

whispering
all night
inside
the zoo
so close
to
you
we
kiss
S U N R I S E

WOMEN VETERINARIANS
Vida

Gorillas watch us.
Sunrise heats us.

I snap a few photos of the apes
while Luci asks me about careers.

She wants to know how difficult it is
to get into veterinary school, and how
will she ever endure the sight of blood,
and what about euthanasia, wouldn't it be
devastating to end the life
of a terminal
patient?

The only question I can answer is the first.
Most states only have one place to study
veterinary medicine, so it's competitive,
but she's smart, and she studies hard.

One hundred years ago there were hardly any
female veterinarians, but now most are women,
the result of laws that protect equality
and girls who grow up fiercely

perseverant
and determined.

My favorite example is Lila Miller,
one of the first Black vet students at Cornell,
who almost gave up her studies because of racism
and a life-threatening allergy to horses.

But Lila persevered, worked at pet shelters,
and transformed them from euthanasia facilities
to sanctuaries for rehabilitation and adoption.

I tell Luci that all it takes is one person's kindness
to completely change the world of creatures,
even though I wonder the same things
about myself—illness, blood, suffering,
and the death of pets,
how could I ever
be as brave as Lila?

STORYTELLING . . .
Vida

is history, like the true tale Islande tells
about 2022, a year when all the birds in every zoo
had to be moved indoors to protect them
from avian flu
spread by contact
with free creatures.

Imagine the challenge—nests and chicks were carried
so carefully, animal keepers desperate to treasure
each rare egg.

Storks in the okapi barn.
Doves housed with butterflies.
Puffins and penguins crowded behind glass.
Flamingos refusing to be separated, so they fluttered
all together, dancing and twirling into a bathroom.

Imagine the joy when finally, during the spring of 2023,
all the birds were returned to outdoor enclosures
with a view of the stormy sky
called survival.

IMPERFECT
Vida

All three of Adán's sisters agree with me
that we are bad feminists, like Roxane Gay,
who wrote about loving dresses, the color pink,
taking care of babies, and other traditions
including the firm belief that carrying spiders
out of a house
is still
men's work.

We want equal opportunities,
not identical memories.

Being imperfect feminists is still so much better
than not being feminists at all, so we keep reading
poetry by Joy Harjo, Maya Angelou, Rita Dove,
and Lucille Clifton, then memoirs by Malala Yousafzai
and Michelle Obama, wondering if maybe
someday we'll be better feminists
who manage to change
our own strange
limitations.

DAYLIGHT
Adán

I spend the morning showing overnight campers
energetic animals who leap with excitement
because they're alive
beneath sunrise
another chance
for the thrill
of exploration
even inside high fences.

Springboks, wallabies, lemurs, singing gibbons,
each effort to levitate reminds me of childhood
with Vida/Serena
mi vida serena
my serene life
rising
toward
sky!

the children
were impatient
all day at school
waiting
waiting
waiting
for their chance
to save a songbird,
a pig, horse, or mule
simply because
they believed
in human kinship
with creatures

IDEAS ARE CREATURES TOO
Adán

When we finally go home after camping
at the zoo, my little sister walks with a cane
instead of riding in her wheelchair.

She announces that she's decided how to cool
Abuelo's rage against Rita, and she knows
that I have to be the one who strives
to change his mind.

A letter.
Snail mail.
Every young person
in both families
will sign!

At first I laugh.
Who writes on paper
instead of texting?

Old folks.
So we try it.
The idea is alive.
Our letter grows like a story.

Each of my sisters adds her own hopes
for peace between las familias
as if Vida and I are Romeo y Julieta
with all our youthful relatives
suddenly united to end an ancient war
by signing a peace treaty
that frees
future generations
from the inherited
curse of hatred.

FORGIVING OUR FAMILY HISTORY
Vida

Photos illustrate your letter about our need
for an end to bitter decades of hostility
that we weren't even aware of
because it started before
we existed.

QUERIDOS
Adán

por favor
nuestro amor
con cariño

All the words we include in the letter
come from gentleness, even though pictures
that Vida prints and seals inside envelopes
show the snarling lips and frantic eyes
of an old man who screamed and shrieked
like a mythical beast, transforming
my eighteenth birthday party
into a monstrosity.

He was justified.
Rita's journalism
caused him pain.

But Rita was right too, the news she investigated
needed to be written and distributed, so the only
real villain in this tragedy
was censorship imposed by tyranny.

UNITY
Vida and Adán

One last photo
goes into the envelope's
written plea.

Flamingos
with clipped wings
as we dance together
human and avian hopes
wildly
free.

MINIMALIST
Vida

sometimes my favorite photos are simple
a single feather or seed, the bird or tree   imagined

just as the essence of love is so easy
whenever it's just you and me   wishing

THE VOICE OF A PHOTOGRAPH
Adán

No one who looks at a picture of us dancing
with pink flamingos
could ever guess that it's a festival
of noise
each bird honk-squawking
like a cross between
a goose
and a crow.

I hope this photo
suggests a vehement protest
just by showing
        our movements
the fierce
            swirls
of energy.

in el monte all the animals knew
that only children could be trusted

the girl and boy roamed courageously
like mythical beings, sometimes soaring
as they rose
above fear

he was a lightning-swift runner
and she had a voice like the sea breeze

together they inspired the confidence
of creatures who galloped or flapped wings
to celebrate
a festive escape
from corrals
and cages

SNAIL MAIL
Adán

I could deliver this letter in person
but today, once again, Abuelo and Papi
are drunk and fighting, so I stamp the envelope,
then drop it off at the post office.

Let it move slowly.
By the time Abuelo reads our words
maybe he'll be sober, finally obeying
doctor's orders to give his mended heart
a chance.

Either way
at least I'm striving
to glide slowly
toward the goal
of peace.

RELUCTANT WARRIOR
Vida

Even though I had to kick and bite to escape
from rapists
I avoid books and movies where girls
have to fight.

My only wish is to make men more peaceful
not to create women who are forced
to become violent.

CHANGE
Adán

Imagine how helpless my little sister would be
if doctors hadn't figured out that polio survivors
can learn how to walk again, with splints, braces,
and the painful effort of physical therapy.

No one should ever
become the victim
of hopelessness.

Even if Abuelo doesn't listen to me this time
I'll keep trying to change his mind
about treasuring the present
instead of raging
about the past.

No young person
should ever have to inherit
ancestral hatred.

FRAMING TIME
Vida

One of Abuelita Rita's most famous photos
shows my grandfather weakened by diabetes
long before I was born.

It was during Cuba's worst era of hunger—no protein
or insulin, even hospitals lacked electricity, no fuel
for an ambulance, only grass to feed horses
who carried Abuelo
slowly.

In the photo, he's surrounded by official
government rations: flour, salt, rice, a few beans,
tobacco, and enough sugar to die swiftly
instead of one bite
at a time.

Now I feel like I'm inside that picture
waiting to see whether the past will crush
my future.

TOO BUSY TO WORRY
Adán

We can't just sit and wait for an answer
to our plea for a family peace treaty,
we have to work every weekday
and on Saturdays we both volunteer
at the wildlife rescue center
and the therapeutic riding stable
plus Vida has photography
while I run, lifts weights,
and practice baseball
with my friends, so time
fades to a whirlwind
of wistfully
anticipated
possibilities.

WE'RE ONLY HUMAN
Vida

Sometimes on Sundays
we escape to a lagoon
so we can volunteer
at a manatee refuge
where gentle creatures
recover from wounds
sliced by the sharp
propellers
of speedboats
that make me wish
I could belong
to a more
peaceful
species.

We're only human
but animals deserve
so much more
kindness.

MENTORSHIP
Vida

At the wildlife rescue center
I read a poem titled "To Be Held"
from a book called *A History of Kindness*
by Linda Hogan, and it seems like each owl,
eagle, raccoon, opossum, and coyote
listens
so carefully
treating me like a mentor.

The verse begins with an embrace by light
and ends with healing after a storm of life.

My own favorite teacher is Dr. Ramos,
the veterinarian who always respects me.

When she volunteers at the zoo, she invites me
to help her examine the flamingos, and suddenly
I remember how the future felt so much bigger
before that attack, at a time when I still
trusted everyone.

FLAMINGO VET CHECK
Vida

I drape a long pink neck
over my shoulder, while Dr. Ramos
checks wings, feet, and vital signs,
then vaccinates against West Nile
and other deadly avian viruses.

Afterward, she suggests
various careers for me—zoo vet,
animal keeper, wildlife photographer
all the adventurous passions I'd already
selected on my own, as if my mentor
is confirming that I have the ability
to study, study, study, learn,
and somehow
at the same time
teach myself
courage.

FLEE!
Adán

A hurricane warning
arrives abruptly
the mandatory evacuation command
repeated everywhere at once—news,
neighbors, relatives, friends
all packing at the same time
with only a few hours left
to drive north
or fly . . .

Rita and Vida are in her car,
while my whole family crowds into
landscape trucks, and we keep in touch
by calling and texting
while the threatening sky
scrambles our messages
creating
chaos.

A NIGHTMARE IN DAYLIGHT
Adán

Dark clouds
     spin
twist
        spit
    hurl
      trash
  branches
        roof tiles
   as we creep north
trapped in traffic
   bumper-to-bumper
some cars   abandoned
   beneath   torrents
while people   shiver
      in
    terror
above floodwaters
     where alligators
and poisonous snakes   writhe.

ROADBLOCK
Adán

The storm path shifts abruptly.
Phone notifications and announcements
from electronic signs above the road
suddenly urge us
to return
home.

Highway patrol cars guide everyone
back the way we came, in order to avoid
driving right into the tricky hurricane.

I try to picture whorls of spiral wind
high above us, but all I can see
in my mind
is the quiet eye of el huracán
        as if the sky
        is studying
           Earth.

EYE OF THE STORM
Adán

       the glare
of   air's
      patient fury

WHY NOT?
Vida

I know that zoo animals
are never evacuated during hurricanes
but still
I wish
I could stay
to offer comfort
food
songs . . .

Next time
there's a storm
I'll volunteer.

Why shouldn't I be
one of the brave keepers
who guards endangered species
when floods grow ferocious
and winds become fierce?

HOME IS A PUZZLE
WITH MISSING PIECES
Adán

After the canceled evacuation
Abuelo finds my letter in the mailbox
and shuts himself in the garage
to drink
and ignore me.

He's still so incredibly angry
about events that have nothing
to do with me
or Vida.

I need a conflict-free place to live
so I move out quietly, accepting Coach's offer
to stay in his pool house, in exchange for
a few hours of landscape gardening.

It's an easy decision
until I think about my little sister,
who still needs me.

RUBBLE
Vida

Each time one of the female gorillas
eats a leaf or fruit, she chants her own quiet
little song of contentment, while gazing at me
as if she's sending an invitation
to join her chorus
so I do what I can to reproduce
wordless music
and together we sing
to the wounded sky
and damaged Earth.

NORMAL IS AN ILLUSION
Adán

Sometimes I feel
like Vida and I are two creatures
from Eden, exiled along with humans
even though we're not the ones
who ate stolen fruit.

Sometimes I feel
like a captive wild canine
pacing back and forth
between stages
of evolution.

PATHWAY
Adán

Coach is just like me
un balsero cubano
only older, calmer, wiser . . .

but when he advises me to forgive my family,
I don't want to listen—all I do is imagine the race
of a ball in midair, as it aims its direction far away
from safety, because leaving home base
is the only way to return
home.

TIMING
Vida

Before Rita retired
Adán could have lived with me
and no one would have noticed
but now we're only together
in front of my abuelita, or at the zoo
with a no-public-display-of-affection rule
for all employees, even those who wear
a jade engagement ring
or a tattooed one.

So we find moments alone
at the wildlife sanctuary
late at night
serenaded
by owls
and coyotes.

Humorous hoots and howls
are melodious accompaniments
for our strange
romance.

FOURTH OF JULY
Adán and Vida

Animals are terrified of fireworks
so we volunteer to stay late at the zoo
helping keepers make sure all the creatures
are safe inside their steel-and-concrete
night houses, the same ones that serve
as shelters
during storms.

In this realm of feathers and hooves
we feel like island children again
rising above a cage
of waves.

WE SING TO DROWN
THE SOUND OF GUNFIRE
Vida

All the animals are hidden now
but we stay, just in case they need
emotional-support humans
to help them
feel safe.

As if fireworks weren't enough noise
on the Fourth of July, bullets explode,
semiautomatic weapons, a war of rage
instead of an old-fashioned celebration.

So we sing all over the zoo
near each sturdy night house,
hoping our feelings of concern
reach the frightened creatures
who huddle inside
screeching their own
wordless music.

the children
moved like silky water
over stones
and mist

then they rose
back up
never
abandoning
any terrified
or wounded creature

CURVEBALL
Adán

we kiss
as if we are clouds
evaporating in sunlight

when scientists try to define love
    by analyzing hormones, pheromones,
        and heart rates, they forget
            that there's no way
              to explain
                the absence
                  of gravity
or predict the path
                      of levitation
and understand where
          our feet might land
            touch soil
              grow
                roots

LOCKS
Vida

The next day
all the females of Adán's family
change the locks on every door of their house.

After a night of turmoil, with men drunk
and fighting, women and girls have given up
on ever convincing them to live peacefully . . .

so as soon as his papi and abuelo fall asleep
in a trailer parked near a Walmart
Adán returns
to his home.

That week at our feminist book club meeting
we read a poem by Joy Harjo
about imagination
being a door.

ALMOST PEACEFUL
Adán

Living at home again is confusing
because Abuelo and Papi are now parked
right outside the house, drinking rum
and inviting me to join them.

In a world
of violent men
I feel like an exile.

GUARDIANS
Adán

The next overnight camp is almost stormy,
so all over the nocturnal zoo, people lie awake
listening to wolves, lions, leopards, and wind.

Children are too scared to roam very far,
but teens start wandering, taunting animals,
tossing trash into enclosures, then laughing
when creatures nibble plastic bags
that could get tangled in their bellies
and become deadly.

We're guardians.
Our uniforms give us the authority
to order people back to their sleeping bags
with instructions to behave like they care
about every living being.

Sometimes humans make me feel ashamed
of our big, intelligent brains and small,
beastly hearts.

FUTURISTIC
Adán

By the next month, love feels light
and our ability to levitate above worries
                    seems so natural.

There's a new conservation center
at the zoo, with climate-action videos,
interactive displays for children,
and an exhibit of photos by Vida.

Eyes, fur, feathers, claws.
Each detail is so emotional
that these framed creatures
look just as real as the ones
outside walls and fences,
in the wild, where animals
depend on humans to end
our destruction
of millions
of species.

FLY, BIRDS, FLY!
Vida

Right before the opening of my photo exhibit
I recite a poem in one of the aviaries,
a verse by Olive Senior
from Jamaica
about bird season
when boys hunt
while girls
stand in
doorways
whispering
urgent
pleas
for
winged beings
to escape
escape
escape!

poetry was at the heart
of all the girl's healing songs
each line a rhythmic plea
for mercy

DESTRUCTION
Adán

Chet shows up while I'm helping Islande and Rita
hang the photographs for Vida's exhibit.

There's an older man with him, his father,
who announces that their surname is now part
of this particular building, because they've made
such a huge donation that all exhibits
are theirs to approve
or reject.

Islande shakes her head, mutters a curse,
and puts her hand on my arm
to keep me calm
as the two men
smash frames
rip photos
and destroy
the captions
that would have
helped children
understand wildlife.

EVIDENCE
Vida

Just outside the doorway
Adán reaches for my shoulders
trying to turn me away from
the sight of bare walls.

Chet approaches me
and spouts advice, telling me I should settle
out of court, but I manage to stay silent
because right behind him, my abuelita is already
circling the room with her powerful camera
documenting a crime for our lawyer—proof
that one of the defendants
in a sexual assault case
is trying to intimidate me—
the plaintiff—who was
still a minor at the time
of the crime.

It feels fair
to imagine Chet and his friends
registered as pedophiles, someday
after they're finally released
from prison.

Three other girls have already agreed
to speak, shout, and testify
that they were raped
by Chet and his buddies.

In my opinion
his hideous father
is equally guilty.

SOLACE
Vida

Late
that night
after anger
and sadness
I sing with owls,
eagles, a bobcat,
and a panther,
our chorus
in a language
we invent
by combining
the musical
ingenuity
of many
species
all of us
kin.

CAPTIONS
Vida

I keep thinking about the descriptions I wrote
for each photo, brief statements to help children
understand the urgent need for conservation.

—Half of all giraffes have disappeared
in just thirty years.

—The reason Andean flamingos are endangered
is cradled in your hand, the battery of your cell phone,
a product of lithium mining in wetlands.

Each caption was intended to help children
make the leap from simple visual images
to an emotional craving
for change.

Now I'll start over, make new prints of photos,
buy frames, rewrite the captions, and add one small
self-portrait, my life story summarized
by a single bold word—*survivor*.

AMBUSH
Vida

Already devastated by the confrontation
with Chet and his father, I don't really want
to attend a fancy dinner with Adán, but his coach
has arranged for him to meet with a pro scout
who plans to talk him out of pursuing college.

He's confused and anxious
so I need to support him.

He's always there for me
when I need encouragement
so why do I feel incapable
of figuring out which dress to wear—
flouncy instead of tight, swishing below the knee,
and not too much cleavage, even the quietly muted
blue-gray sombra de palma print of shady leaves
looks like something my abuelita would have worn
fifty years ago
instead of now.

I wish I could wrap myself in a real forest
like a solitary orangutan on her way
to climb a tall tree

and build
a safe
nest
alone.

Soledad.
That's how I feel.
Loneliness in a crowd seems unreasonable
but the scouts and coaches and players
are all drinking—Adán and I are the only
sober ones.

When a stranger pretends to plant friendly
besitos on my cheeks as a greeting, I resist.

Then he grips my chin
and swerves his lips to my mouth
in a movement that I can only describe
as invasive.

NO
Vida

I hear my voice
emerge from my throat
as a growl.
NO.

But the invader of my mouth
does not seem to hear me
until Adán
and his coach
both repeat what I said.
No. She said no. Listen.

Women's words are just a drifting mist
that passes through some men's minds
formless.

SWEET SPOT
Adán

There's a sturdy place
near a baseball bat's center of mass
where vibrations are minimal.

You can find it by tapping with a hammer.
The sweet spot feels solid, like a stud in a wall.
It gives the ball a launch angle of
eight to thirty-two degrees.
Precise.
Predictable.
Combined with velocity
it yields a hard hit.

Why can't human behavior
be quantifiable too, with mathematical rules,
so I can be prepared for surprises?

The scout who kissed Vida caught me off guard.
Imagine how much more shocked she must have been!
Even past experience with aggressiveness never really
prepares anyone for an attack, so I need a sweet spot
for understanding my own reactions.

EXIT
Vida

I leave the restaurant.
No explanation needed.
Everyone witnessed the crime
because even
one tiny
unwanted kiss
is sexual assault.

Tomorrow I'll file a complaint
with the offender's employer.

Tonight
all I want to do
is go back to the wildlife sanctuary
where I can feel a sense of belonging.
When Adán tries to come with me
I ask him for space, and he listens,
but as soon as I'm alone with owls
and crows, I find myself wishing
to reach for his hand, our minds
entwined.

IMMENSITY
Adán

I feel the way I did when baseball rules changed
and the size of bases grew so huge
that anything seemed
possible.

Will Vida blame me for the actions of other men
or can she still see me
as myself?

I resisted hitting the guy who kissed her
even though walking away
required all my
willpower.

Now I crave closeness
and she's the one who's acting ghostly.

One text is all I get, just a brief request
for patience, as if I can pull the whole sky
into my heart, and make my endurance

endless.

SPACE
Vida

I
asked
for
space
but
now
all
I want
is closeness
your voice   scent   touch
so I venture away from safety
back to the world of humans
all my owls and other animal friends
patiently waiting to hear
my next
song.

VOLUNTEERS ARE URGENTLY NEEDED
Adán

The call for zoo employees willing to stay
comes as a phone message, along with a warning
that catastrophic gusts are approaching—winds
far beyond a Category 5 hurricane's
157-miles-per-hour threshold.

This storm could reach twice that level,
a disaster recorded only once, when Hurricane Samuel
struck Cozumel, Mexico, in 2020, at 300 mph.
It hardly made the news, because most of the torment
was at sea and on small islands, not a big city like Miami
with millions of people who need to evacuate swiftly
despite traffic, a frenzy, panic, desperation,
and the refusal to believe
that shrieking

      storms

   are

more

  and more dangerous

each

year.

HURRICANE ZOO
Vida

I'll stay with creatures
who need to be protected
by concrete and steel
inside sturdy night houses
sharing the dangers of hope.

RECONCILIATION
Adán

I won't leave without you, Vida.
My whole familia is already packing
to evacuate, and your abuelita
is going with my mother, because somehow
all their old resentments have now
fallen away, replaced by memories
of friendship on the island
long ago.

All it takes to end a feud between neighbors
is this new form of measureless danger—climate
terror.

MOBILIZING AN ENTIRE ZOO
Vida

I feel like we're living in a horror movie.
How can so many creatures be moved indoors
so quickly, and what about the wildlife sanctuary,
all those animals are relatively small, can they
be transported in crates loaded onto trailers?
I just pray that Dr. Ramos has enough volunteers . . .

Islande assigns me to the commissary,
an enormous kitchen where I help prepare meals
as well as treats to tempt all the creatures
into their impenetrable night houses.

Hippos will have watermelons to smash.
Elephants need so much foliage that branches
and hay bales are hauled with heavy equipment.

Squirming mice, worms, and crickets, the live food
for reptiles and rodents, make me feel cruel
even though I know there's no way to avoid
the life-and-death nature
of predation.

SEPARATED
Adán

While you work in the kitchen
I drive a truck to round up hoofed animals
and herd them toward safety.

Even the strongest bison and bighorn sheep
look so fragile, bones hidden within muscles
just as vulnerable
as my own.

Soon trees will be uprooted, roofs will soar
like paper, and a surge of waves could bring the ocean
flowing toward us . . .

If only we could be together right now.

I promise I'll find a way
to join you, wherever you end up—
in that sturdy bathroom with flamingos,
or behind the lions' den, the gorillas,
even a delicate aviary would feel safer
with you than alone.

BOTANICAL CHALLENGE
Adán

As I lure herds toward safety
by driving slowly, with a load of hay
to tempt them, I wave to gardeners
who are leaving, unable to protect
trees and shrubs.

Landscaping inside animal enclosures
is so specialized that I've never really
considered all the intricacies—leaves
and flowers can't be poisonous to animals,
but they shouldn't be too palatable either,
or they'll be devoured completely
so a compromise is needed
between safety
and survival.

Maybe that's what you and I need, mi vida,
some sort of halfway mark to help us
face danger without losing hope—our minds
can grow like vines with blossoms
that drink from deep roots.

SURREALISTIC
Vida

I'm assigned to a men's bathroom
in a concrete-and-steel building
with fifty Caribbean flamingos,
all the beautiful pink birds
staring
at themselves
in a mirror
heads tilted
flirting.

I fill all three sinks with water
and cover the floor with straw,
then pour shrimp smoothies
from a blender into bowls
that send the excited birds
swirling.

When they bend long necks
I marvel at their flexibility.
Flamingos have nineteen vertebrae
while giraffes—just like humans—possess
only seven.

I wish my mind contained the equivalent
ability to bend, reach, and twist, so I could see
around doors and over walls, all the way
to wherever you are, Adán—in the elephant barn
or that tunnel behind leopard dens, or maybe
you're still in one of the aviaries, with delicate
                        latticework roofs that might already
be blowing away while you rescue
                        birds of paradise
and hornbills.

There's nothing to do but wait.
I have a cot, blanket, first aid kit,
protein shakes, dehydrated meals,
my phone, and just in case
it stops working, a radio
of the sort used by police
and firemen, because we
are an emergency service
for zoo animals,
their only link
to the unknown
future.

If this hurricane
grows too powerful for survival,
you and I might die right beside
our beloved
creatures.

I only hope that by then
we'll find each other and be
together.

For now, I hold my breath and listen
to the awkward squawks
of gracefully dancing
miraculous
birds.

FLAMINGO BALANCE
Vida

long beaks

sinuous

pink

necks

delicate

feathers

harshly

clipped

wings

stilt

legs

dance

above

strong

webbed

feet

so far beneath the freedom of sky
their world is now a muddy shore
of submerged wishes

VIGIL IN THE ZOO NURSERY
Adán

After rounding up wildebeest, water buffalo,
camels, llamas, alpacas, and mountain goats,
I'm finally seated in a safe shelter
with baby animals and their keepers,
my mind sliding back and forth
between the sweet eyes
of a newborn chimp
whose captive-born mother
doesn't know how to feed him—
and you, Vida, waiting with flamingos
while we text encouraging emojis
as if this is an ordinary workday
instead of the strongest hurricane
ever to strike
anywhere
on Earth.

Soon the storm's quiet eye will swoop
above us, and I'll have my only chance
to leave this refuge, and run to join you!

the first creature
                the children ever rescued
                        was a lost puppy frightened
                        by thunder
during the second half of un huracán
after the silent eye had passed
and true fury
crashed
onto
land

VIGIL WITH FLAMINGOS
Vida

The stench of shrimp, guano, and feathers
doesn't disturb me, I'm often so close to wildlife odors
that my clothes and hair hardly ever smell clean,
but when I discover a dark chocolate bar
in my emergency kit
childhood
pours
over
me
as I remember your friendship
and our secretive rescue of creatures
in the cacao forest, where I knew
there would always be one human
who could understand
our hybrid blend
of fear
    and
       joy.

You put this candy here—you planned
this aromatic surprise.

KINDNESS IS A SPARK OF LIGHT
Vida

just enough joy
to flood the dark storm
with sunlight

FRAGMENTED MESSAGE
Adán

your last text
before the phones
and radios
fail
says you're safe
and moving toward me
so I answer with flamingo noise
because I can't find human words
and I know you'll listen
for as long as possible
even though
my own voice
is silenced by fear
as I picture you
levitating
high above
the storm's
force

I AM NOT IN THE HURRICANE'S EYE
Adán

The storm's path must have swerved
west to the Gulf Coast
or south toward Cuba
because once again
we've been spared
at least
for now

                as I pick my way

     through ruins   of broken fences

          uprooted trees   and

              fragile walls . . .

When I finally reach you
we embrace
so tightly
that
no
wind
could
ever separate
our   soaring   imaginations

EACH KISS LIFTS US . . .
Vida and Adán

into a sky
of islands
above islands
love
within
love

TEN HOURS LATER
Adán and Vida

The zoo is a reborn
hurricane world
of super-alive
survivors.

As humans roam
the enclosures
repairing
damage
kindness
sends sparks of light
into the night houses
where animals await
our mystical belief
in hope
hope
hope.

AUTHOR'S NOTE

Island Creatures is a work of fiction. The wildlife sanctuary and breeding zoo are not based on real institutions. However, parts of the story were inspired by my own experiences with animals in Cuba and in the United States.

I have been fortunate enough to work behind the scenes for an irrigation water conservation project at a breeding zoo near San Diego. I also attended many classes at the San Diego Zoo, where my daughter and I camped overnight outside the gorilla enclosure, made Popsicles for elephants, fed carrots to rhinos, and learned how to pet hedgehogs.

In the southern United States, most zoos never evacuate animals during hurricanes. There are famous photos of flamingos in a bathroom at Zoo Miami during Hurricane Andrew in 1992 and Hurricane Georges in 1998. That particular zoo now has a special storm shelter for flamingos, but smaller zoos—like the fictional one in this book—continue to improvise.

The feminist book club was inspired by the consciousness-raising groups of the 1970s, where young men—including the one who became my husband—advocated equal rights for women. Rita's dilemma is also one that I have shared in my daily life. Every time a Cuban or Cuban American journalist, novelist, or poet writes about the island, we realize that friends and relatives might be punished for reading our words in a land of strict censorship and harsh penalties. Dengue fever epidemics are one of the many subjects that have been suppressed by censors.

Many other details in this novel are inspired by scientific facts. For instance, cacao is a tree native to mountainous regions of the tropical Américas, where climate change endangers the future of chocolate. Andean flamingos are one of many wetland species threatened by the lithium mining needed for electric car batteries. My sister had polio as a child. As an adult, she worked hard to become an excellent equestrian and skier. Polio is now a preventable disease, but many parents have decided not to vaccinate their children.

Vida and Adán came to me as fully formed, complex individuals. They refused to let me rest until I had written their love story. They hope you find it hopeful.

All over the world, violence against women is an ongoing horror. Many girls and women never speak about crimes against us, but silence only makes the problem more difficult to solve. If you or anyone you know needs to report sexual violence, you can find help at rainn.org.

ACKNOWLEDGMENTS

I thank God for people who believe in kindness. I'm grateful to my family, especially my husband, Curt Engle, who told me he was a feminist on the day that I met him and has always remained dedicated to equality and fairness for women, as well as kindness to animals.

Special thanks to the San Diego Zoo and Safari Park, and to my daughter, Nicole, and son, Victor, for letting me accompany them to Zoo Camps when they were little.

I'm profoundly grateful to my wonderful agent, Michelle Humphrey; my extraordinary editor, Reka Simonsen; editorial assistant, Jin Soo Chun; and the entire Atheneum publishing team.